DEATH OF A FAMILY LEGACY

RC MERRELL

All rights reserved. No part of this book may be reproduced, scanned or distributed in any form, including digital and electronic or mechanical, including photocopying, recording, or by any information storage and retrieval system, without the prior consent of the author, except for brief quotes for use in reviews.

This book is a work of fiction. Characters, names, places and incidents either are the product of the author's imagination or are used fictitiously, and any resemblance to any actual persons, living or dead, events, or locales is entirely coincidental.

Rcmerrell55@gmail.com - all comments or suggestions / feedback / future book information / send reviews

<u>Books by RC Merrell</u>

<u>Morrelli Private Investigative Series:</u>
    #1: Chrysalis Expedition
    #2: Chrysalis Nightmare
    #3: Recycling Day
    #4: Death of a Family Legacy

<u>The Morrelli Chronicles:</u>
    #1: School Bus Driver

__To Ben:__

My cousin Ben was taken from this world far too early by the phenomenon that brought the world to its knees: COVID-19! Ben is now gone and everyone who knew him will live with this loss. I was one of those fools, who did not listen to life's messages, and after his death I came to the revelation that Ben was not just my cousin; Ben was also my friend. It saddens me that I just now verbalized this fact. Don't make my mistake; hold your family and friends close, because you never know what tomorrow brings.

__Acknowledgments__

__Sheri Merrell__ – *My every breath in this world. Sheri not only reads, corrects and re-reads, she listens to my thoughts, encourages my writing and is my inspiration every step of the way.*

__Chuck Roberts__ -- **__Editor__** – *Chuck has freely given his time and expertise to this writing endeavor that I embarked upon later in life. Although I consider myself a writer, I find it difficult to put into words what an integral part of this process Chuck is for me. Even that sounds clinical and monotone. You are truly a kind human being who gives his time to family, friends, strangers and anyone in need. I am blessed to be part of your family and friend world.*

CHAPTER 1

Activity and anxiety levels were high inside the small rented building. Computers were humming, printers were spitting out volumes of paper, and people were busy working everywhere. The opposite was true outside the confines of this rented space. Very little activity was normal in the quaint mountain town of Crenna, Maine. Crenna was surrounded by woods, mountains and crystal clear lakes. One of these lakes was beautifully located in the center of the town. The lake was the physical center as well as the center of many of the town's activities. Fishing, picnicking, sunbathing, family gatherings, carnivals, church events, and so much more took place around this beautiful body of water. The town sat so high in the mountains that on a crisp fall morning the clouds were low enough to surround the town in a beautiful white mist. It was as if you were walking inside the clouds. Some people felt it was eerie looking, but most embraced its beautiful feeling of being enveloped inside a soft protected pillow.

On a clear summer night the stars and moon would light the little town with a comforting soft glow. It was a perfect-picture postcard that the townspeople lived in each and every day.

Crenna was an old logging town named after Abner Crenna, or Abe as he was known to the locals. Abe was one of the early pioneers of logging. He came to the area alone, eventually bringing his immediate family. He worked day and night to grow his one-man logging effort into a vast logging empire. As his workload outgrew him, Abe began bringing family into the area to help. It was not long before others got word of the growth in this remote area. Stores, bars, barbers and more came to start their businesses in this new town appointed Crenna, Maine. Abe's logging business flourished for many, many years.

After Abe passed away, many of his descendants stayed in the area, continued working in the logging business, and in some cases started their own businesses to support the logging industry. Paul Crenna was Abe's oldest son, and took over the logging business. It could not have been a worse time to be responsible for the Crenna logging empire. Their little corner of paradise was on life support, for a wide array of reasons.

The town was dying a slow painful death like many other cities and towns across America. The three main culprits were Omicron, the Green movement, and the elimination of paper as we know it. Omicron became the ruler of our free country, being at the center of all governmental policies. Wearing a mask became the norm. Forced vaccinations resulted in a smaller workforce as people quit their jobs rather than put an unknown chemical into their body, and could do so on a nicely increased unemployment payment. Businesses closed when they could not get workers; supply chain interruptions only added to these store closures. All of these impacted the small town of Crenna. The government's Green agenda was not supportive of logging, which was also beginning to impact the industry. Probably the biggest impact was the invention of plastic paper. It had the look and feel of paper, and did not smear as one would think. People were being encouraged to eliminate paper towels in the kitchen and bidets were becoming a fixture in every home. The perfect storm was brewing directly over the logging industry.

Crenna was fighting both a loss of workers, and a loss of demand. The loss of workers was outpacing the loss of demand.

Compounding the problem was the lack of truck drivers, so the logs were not getting to market.

First, two of the newer restaurants were forced to close due to lack of employees, not to mention reduced revenue. Then one of the larger bars closed, followed by one of the two motels in town. Smaller businesses like gift shops, bed and breakfasts, bakeries, were also closing, leaving empty buildings everywhere. The town was looking deserted; if this desertion continued, it would surely become a ghost town, and the Crenna legacy would die.

Paul Crenna was watching his family's legacy fade away under his leadership. Paul had earned the family trait of being a fighter; he would not lie down and just let this happen. The problem was that his fight was fueled by anger, as opposed to love and concern for his neighbors and their families. Crenna hated these people who were leaving, or sitting at home collecting government money instead of working. His hatred for the government and the disloyal workers consumed him, which clouded his judgment and made him unable to focus on viable solutions. Paul had amassed quite a fortune and had decided to waste it on revenge rather than working to find a way out of this mess.

Crenna had attended a very prestigious college for a degree in business to give him the knowledge he required to take over the logging company. He did very well in his studies, but learned that his real passion was for computers. He had really blossomed into a computer genius. Yes he ran the company, but computers made him complete. It was through this all consuming passion that he would execute his vengeance. Crenna's first thought was revenge through Omicron, but he recognized the Omicron factor dictating government policy would soon wane due to a rapid rise in public discontent. The government would have to reverse its course of control through this virus.

In another part of town, Liam Kelly (Red) wondered if he had made the right choice moving to this quiet, scenic area. About a year ago, Red had decided to take the position of town Sheriff, recently vacated by a friend who had fought next to him in Afghanistan. Red, his wife Alannah, and their daughter Elmear, packed up everything, and made the move across country. They wanted their daughter to grow up in the confines of a smaller, safer town. When they first arrived, moved in and Red started his job, they were elated by their decision. Life was good in small town America. This feeling didn't last long as things around town were beginning to change, and not for the better. Crime was increasing, tensions were high, and Paul Crenna was not helping to calm things down. Now Red found himself at odds with the most powerful force in town, the town's namesake, the Crenna family. Should they cut and run to find another small town and begin their dreams all over again? This was not something Red, or Alannah, wanted to do. They decided to fight to bring this town back to the idyllic place they had moved to just a short time ago.

CHAPTER 2

Paul Crenna's personality and demeanor had been changing rapidly. He had gone from a calm rational husband, father, and boss, to a hot-headed, irrational bastard. His family life went from full throttle participation, to him rarely showing up at home or to family events. When he did come home, Paul was drunk and verbally abusive to his wife Lily, who shielded this from their children, Randy and Abigail. At first, it was mainly verbal abuse. Eventually Paul turned physical, pushing Lily around and demanding sex.

Lily was a seemingly sweet, demure woman who grew up far from the town of Crenna. She was loved by everyone in town, and always helped her neighbors. She raised her two children, and still had time for community outreach almost every day.

By no stretch of the imagination did demure mean she was not able to take care of herself. Paul and Lily used to hunt, fish, camp, and she was even known to be outside in the middle of the logging action during her younger years.

Their daughter Abigail had just graduated high school and was headed off to nursing school. A nurse was something Lily had always wanted to become. Lily was so very proud when Abigail told her mother that nursing would be her career path. Abigail was very popular with high school boys, who continually competed for her affection. She was not interested in any of them for a few reasons; first and foremost, watching her parents' relationship deteriorate in front of her eyes was heartbreaking. She had been daddy's little girl for many years, but now there were days she hated this unknown man. Secondly, she wanted to go to college with no strings, meet new people, have fun and dig into her nursing studies. She became very close to her mom, because Abigail knew her mother was suffering the loss of what used to be a loving husband. In reality there was also a third reason. She wanted to escape the toxic relationship that was her family, and truth be told, her mother wanted this for her as well.

Randy, their son, was older, and out of the house. Because he was not living the family stress every day, as was Abigail, he had a slightly different view of his father. Following in his father's footsteps, Randy studied and worked to become a computer programming expert. He had actually created an algorithm that provided traffic speed deterrents which, if approved, would change the structure of police departments. Focusing on driving being a privilege, not a right, this algorithm would utilize the car's computer system to issue tickets and control traffic. Technology embedded in the road would analyze the speed of a vehicle. A predetermined distance down the road, additional technology would either ignore the vehicle or send a signal to the car slowing it down, alerting the driver to pull over. The driver would pull over at the designated automatic ticketing station. At the station, the driver had two choices: pay or set a court date. Once the traffic encounter was closed in the system, the car's computer would then reset, and the vehicle could continue on its journey. Naturally, emergency vehicles would be outfitted with a bypass system which allowed them to do their job at high speeds when necessary. This would take police out of most traffic patrols, allowing them to focus on real crime.

This invention was important to Randy's path in life. If it were approved and put into action, computer programming and inventing would become his main career, not logging. Right now he was pushing his creation, learning the logging business and becoming actively involved in his father's pursuit to punish the American government.

One Friday evening Lily received a phone call from her husband Paul.

"Lil, my new hundred thousand dollar truck won't start. I'm at the Southern logging office. Any chance you can come pick me up, and I will have the dealership pick up my truck tomorrow?"

There was definite hesitation in Lily's response because typically Friday was a drinking night for Paul.

"Well, ummmm, okay I will be there in about twenty minutes," replied Lily.

She pocketed her taser and headed out to pick him up. It was dark, and at this time of night, she may be the only person on this logging road. It would be a spooky ride to most people, but Lily was a mountain girl so she was actually enjoying the solitude of the ride. She arrived in around twenty minutes as she had told Paul. Lily rounded the last corner on the desolate road, and saw Paul in her vehicle's headlights. He was doing the "drunk lean" against a large pile of neatly stacked logs. The "drunk lean" had Paul swaying against the logs in an attempt to keep his body upright. This was a big indicator to her that he was in fact drunk. Lily slowly moved the car towards Paul, and then turned the vehicle so the passenger door was facing him. Paul kept his position and continued to lean akimbo against the logs.

Lily rolled down the car window and heard him say, "Grab a flashlight. I dropped my wallet."

Again, with much hesitation she did as he demanded. Lily was now positive Paul was drunk as was typical on a Friday night. She walked up to him and trouble immediately started.

"Remember when we used to work the logging office together. After everyone was gone we'd come outside and make love under the blanket of millions of stars. I miss those days baby."

He moved in and tried to hug her, which would not have worked even if he had not been intoxicated. Lily shoved him away, asked him to stop being crazy and get into the car so they could leave. This infuriated him and he lurched forward to grab her. With no time to grab her taser, she powered her foot into his groin, making him crash into the huge pile of logs behind him. In the blink of an eye this body slam destabilized the massive pile, and caused the logs to fall everywhere burying Paul underneath.

Lily jumped out of the way and as she hit the ground she caught a glimpse of a figure running from the area into the woods. Lily quickly jumped up and ran to see if she could make out who the figure was, but it was too dark and the person moved too fast. Whoever the mystery person was, they were now gone and it suddenly hit her that Paul had to be dead underneath that pile of logs. Lily knew she should be doubled over in grief, but she was not one to fake her emotions. She was simply void of emotion.

Lily immediately called Red to come to the Southern logging office, after briefly explaining the situation over the phone. While waiting for Red, she ran the scenario through her head multiple times. Suddenly an oddity came to light in her mind. Paul was very safety conscious and demanded the same from all of his employees. That being said, she wondered why the pile of logs was not secured as procedure dictated. Each completed pile was to be chained to prevent logs from rolling everywhere. The pile that fell on Paul was not chained, and had been an accident waiting to happen.

CHAPTER 3

Earlier that day Paul had spent quite a bit of time in the building he had rented for his computer repair business. The activity inside was at frenzied levels as Paul's ultimate plan for revenge was coming to fruition. The store front had a sign indicating computer repair, which was true, but in reality all the computer, and brain power inside the store was for Paul's diabolical plan to cripple America. Every man and woman working in this building was sick of government control, and was completely loyal to Paul's cause. Their mission statement read, *"Plunge America into a chaotic state, creating a breeding ground for revolution. We must completely break down our country, and then rebuild America back to the America envisioned by our forefathers."*

Inside one of the offices within the rented building, Paul met with his son Randy, and their main programmer Boris Mertvago. Also in attendance, via video conference, was Doctor Svetlana

Vladmelov. Doctor Vladmelov had been the face of American governmental medical policy during the recent Omicron virus scare in America. Even though Svetlana was a government official, she also had good reasons to be part of Crenna's rebellious group. Naturally, her personal gain was the first reason, and the hefty payday from Paul served her well. Creating chaos and conflict in America would gain her much favor with her home country whose goal was to see America fall and democracy crumble.

"Svetlana, we need a full court press on wearing masks and vaccine mandates. You have the teachers union in your pocket; you have convinced big business to support these mandates. Now take it to more grassroots levels. For example, add churches and other nonprofit organizations to these mandates. Spread the word that they will lose their nonprofit exemption if they do not enforce masks and vaccination mandates. You are doing a great job! We can see tensions rising, but let's take it up another notch," Paul demanded as he gave her a wink.

Svetlana was a very desirable, exotic woman, and Paul had met with her privately on many occasions. Paul had a wife, and Svetlana had a powerfully jealous husband, but they managed to maintain a secret relationship during this stressful time. Everyone in this building knew of their rendezvous, but they also knew to keep their mouths closed.

Boris orchestrated the hacking and manipulation of many government elections in the United States. His brain was a computer, and he was revered in the hacking underworld. Boris was yet another member of Crenna's team who was raised in another land, and was taught that America was an enemy, and its destruction was necessary. Working with Paul, Boris would accomplish the biggest hack of all.

Paul's theory of hacking was revolutionary. Traditional hacking pits human against human, meaning someone programs a computer to hack into another computer system, programmed by another human to stop hackers. Paul and his team would pit computer against human. He had created a system that would link with the government's computer as if it were its partner. Instead of fighting against a programmer's defense strategy, their system would become part of the defense system, part of the very computer logic it was planning to infect. Basically, Crenna's system would become a mirror image with multiple layers of programming. While it sounded like a simplistic approach, in reality it was a very complicated, complex algorithm.

When Paul began putting this team together, each one he tried to recruit had to first be convinced his theory would work. Even his son Randy was originally a non-believer.

"Conceptually, it's way too simple, and yet operationally it's way too complex to accomplish," the prospective programmers all proclaimed.

"Mirroring a system is easy. Creating a hidden operating system within a system is difficult, but very doable. For example, we mirror the financial system so it continually shows average historical spending. This creates normalcy to anyone monitoring this portion of the government's vast computerized system. Next we go in and manage money to and from Americans in a manner that creates hostility. This movement of money will be undetectable until the funds are exhausted," Paul summarized to his potential team members.

It was difficult to achieve, but eventually Paul had his dream team, and they had been hard at work for some time now.

"Boris, have we solved the startup issue?" Paul asked.

With all this intricate programming, they had one glitch left to resolve. When the two systems merge, there will be a system hiccup, or blinking if you will. Picture the movies that show someone tapping into a video. The video blinks before settling to the programmed video loop. It's the same issue, and if not resolved, they will be shut down before they even get started.

"We are close, but still have issues. This is truly our biggest challenge, but rest assured we will get it resolved," replied Boris in his deep raspy voice.

"We go 'live' in just a short time, so this needs to be resolved soon! Keep at it day and night," demanded Paul.

Boris did not take kindly to Paul's demands, or for that matter, to Paul in any form. He did not like his entitled American attitude, or his arrogance and demanding tone of late. He had to obey with eagerness, as failure would surely result in his handlers eliminating him. Boris would listen to Crenna for now, but after this was all over, Pauly boy might be in line for a serious accident.

Randy was quiet through the entire meeting. His job was that of a sponge. He was to learn and comprehend everything that was going on, which provided the mission human capital redundancy.

Any human loss, failure or gap, including his father's, would be effectively handled by Randy.

CHAPTER 4

"There has been an accident at the Southern logging office. Paul Crenna was seriously hurt and may be dead. Lily Crenna called it in because she was there when the accident occurred. I have to get out to the scene to see what's going on. I will call later to let you know what's happening. Love you two," Red explained as he hugged his wife Alannah and kissed the head of his daughter, Elmear.

"Be careful. We love you!" Alannah replied, as Red was on his way out the door.

Red already had an ambulance on the way to the scene. This little town had no real crime unit or coroner's department. Red and his deputy Asadi were the entire Crenna Sheriff's department. Until lately, two men were usually sufficient to handle the minor crimes around the normally peaceful town.

In addition to the ambulance, Red contacted Asadi, also sending him to the accident scene. Asadi Zawar was part of the recent airlift of Americans, and their partners, out of his war-torn country of Afghanistan. Asadi had served as an Afghani interpreter with Red's unit during the war in Afghanistan. Red and Asadi had become good friends during their time together in this far away land. When Asadi came to America, Red and Alannah began helping him assimilate into American society. When he was asked, Asadi jumped at the chance to become Red's deputy. Asadi had gone from dodging bullets to dodging leaves as they wafted to the ground in this safe, small mountain town.

Red arrived on scene first and saw Lily frantically trying to move logs that would have been impossible for anyone to move by hand. The first thing Red noticed about Lily was that she appeared emotionless. Lily did not look upset, but rather had the look of determination to push something that ten men could not have moved by hand.

"Lily, please stop. First of all, you are going to hurt yourself. These logs cannot be moved without machinery. Second, this is a crime scene. If Paul is under that pile of logs there is no chance he survived," Red explained.

"I know Red, but I just could not sit here and do nothing. After I notified you, I called our foreman to get him out here to run the equipment to help move these logs. He should be here very soon," replied Lily.

"So tell me what happened, Lily. Start from the beginning," Red stated.

Lily explained everything from Paul's phone call, to her drive out to the office, to Paul's state of mind when she arrived at the office.

"After the accident, I realized the logs had not been secured, which is out of the ordinary as safety conscious as Paul was. I know I saw someone run from behind the logs as they fell. Why would someone be out here in the dark hiding from Paul? Seems odd this freak accident occurred, and then I saw someone running towards the woods in that direction," explained Lily as she pointed towards the woods.

"I would agree Lily, it does seem very odd. While on the surface this seems like a tragic accident, I'm now wondering if it's something more. With your observation about the safety chain missing, and your sighting of another person, this incident may move into the category of a homicide. Is there anyone you know of that may want Paul dead? I also have to be honest, and tell you that we will have to check out your story as part of the investigation," replied Paul.

"I am sure our marital decline will be discussed during this investigation, but while I have grown to hate him, I could never kill him if that's what you are thinking. Paul has made quite a few enemies recently, but I cannot imagine they hated Paul enough to kill him," stated Lily.

Just then the ambulance and Asadi arrived. The EMTs quickly moved their equipment from the ambulance, but could do nothing until the foreman arrived to move the logs. Everyone just had to be patient until Paul's body was uncovered.

"Asadi, as you drove in on the main road, there were two cutoffs the trucks use to bring the logs out of the woods. We have an unknown person who fled the scene into the woods. They may have hid their vehicle on one of these logging roads, giving them a means of escaping the area. Head back to these roads, and see what you can find. Be careful," Red stated.

"Will do Red," Asadi replied as he jumped back into his car and headed back down the main road to find the two logging roads.

Crenna's logging foreman arrived, and quickly moved the machine into position. Carefully, he began moving the heavy logs out of the way. It was a tedious, calculated process, because they really did not know exactly where Paul was located underneath the mess. One by one, the logs were moved, and with each log Lily's stress and anxiety level grew. She knew what she saw, and Paul had to be under the pile. All of a sudden, the reality of the tragedy came to light; when the next log was lifted, it exposed Paul's lifeless, crushed body. Red surveyed the area around Paul, then approved the EMTs to move in to be sure he was dead, as everyone suspected. After determining Paul was in fact dead, they backed off, allowing Red to make a closer examination of the crime scene.

Red bent down to examine the crushed body and took note of the real cause of death. Right away Red noticed a bullet hole in one side of his head, with yet another bullet hole on the other side of his head. One hole seemed to be the entry wound, and the other was probably the exit wound. The gunshot had to have occurred before the pile collapsed or as the logs were falling, because such a wound could not have occurred while Paul was underneath the logs. The town of Crenna had its first murder to investigate!

Red went to examine the logs that had been near Paul's body. He was looking for a hole where the bullet may have entered the wood after exiting Paul's head. Finding the bullet may lead them to the murder weapon.

"Paul, what are you looking for?" asked Lily, as she walked in Red's direction.

Paul stood up saying, "Lily, do not come any closer. As I already told you, this is a crime scene and I am looking for any possible evidence."

"What evidence could there possibly be? The man was crushed by a pile of logs, isn't that evidence enough?" Lily said as she was becoming more and more agitated, and yet still exhibited no signs of grief. Still no tears!

"Paul was shot so please back off and let me do my job," Red informed her in a more demanding tone.

Lily's expression was one of shock, because she now realized it was not an accident. Paul's death was a murder, just as Red had suspected!

CHAPTER 5

Asadi's car moved slowly down the mountain road until he saw a rough path that looked like it could be a logging road. This road was not meant for car use, but Asadi had to see what, or who, might be in the woods. To Asadi, it was the slowest mile he had ever traveled. He was constantly dodging tree roots, stones, holes and at times even small trees that arched low over the roadway. The logging trucks were like tanks and probably just blew through, and over all this debris. He reached the end of the logging road and saw no vehicle, so Asadi headed back out the rough road. When he reached the main road, Asadi turned onto the road and drove for about a mile where he found the second logging path Red had told him about. Once again, Asadi found himself driving down a rough rutted path through the woods. Asadi reached the end of the second road, turned around, and headed back towards the main road. There were no vehicles or humans anywhere in the area.

Asadi missed seeing a huge tree root on his way out. As the front wheel hit the root, his car's front end took a violent bounce upwards. Asadi's head slammed against the driver's seat headrest. Hitting this root literally saved his life because, had his head not bounced against the headrest, a bullet would have pierced his brain. Asadi slammed the car into park, threw open the car door, and rolled out staying flat to the ground. Bullets continued to shatter windows, and cut through the car's metal exterior. The gunshots were silent until they made contact with the car. To Asadi, it appeared there was more than one shooter, because the bullets were hitting the rear, and passenger sides of the car. He slowly moved into the woods using the military crawl. Once deep enough into the woods, Asadi began moving quicker in an upright, but crouched running position. He could hear bullets continuing to hit the glass and metal of his car as he moved away from the scene. When Asadi felt he was far enough away from the gunfire, he called Red on his cell phone.

"Did you find anything?" Red asked.

Whispering into the phone Asadi responded, "Red, speak quietly we have company! My car is being riddled with bullets. I escaped into the woods. I will head out onto the main road. Please meet me where it intersects the second logging road. From what little I can tell, we are dealing with pros here, maybe of sniper caliber."

"I am on my way. Hang tight Asadi," Red replied.

"Get into the office everyone. We have shooters in the woods, and I have to assist my deputy who is taking fire. Lock the door, keep the lights off and stay hidden until we return. Do not open the door until you hear my voice," Red told Lily and everyone else at the scene.

Red quickly jumped into his squad car and raced towards Asadi. When he reached the intersection, sure enough Asadi came out of the woods, and jumped into the passenger seat.

"I think there is more than one shooter. They must have sniper rifles with silencers, and they are marksmen. Had it not been for a major bump in the road causing my head to move backwards, the first shot would have taken me out. As I began driving back up the logging path leading to the main road, one of the shooters seemed to be somewhere on my right side. After the first few shots, gunfire also began hitting the rear section of the car. I did not observe any vehicles or people. I'm all in for a gunfight, but going back there now would be suicide. I cannot tell you exactly where they are, or even how many," explained Asadi.

"We have to get back to the crime scene to keep Lily and the others safe," Red shouted as he spun the car around and sped back towards the logging office.

When they reached the logging office, things got even more chaotic. They exited the car to the sounds of a small helicopter headed their way. In seconds, it was hovering over the area, and gunfire erupted from the open side door. Red and Asadi returned fire from the ground, and continued to fire into the night sky towards the outline of the flying war machine. The helicopter stopped shooting, changed position, and began its frenzied shooting once again. Suddenly, there was a cry of pain from the helicopter, followed by a loud thud on the ground. Someone from the helicopter had fallen and hit the ground. The gunfire from the helicopter went from aiming shots at Red and Asadi, to shooting at whoever had just fallen from the sky. This victim was executed by their own people to make sure death would keep them quiet.

"What have we gotten ourselves into? These people are ruthless, and must be stopped, but who are they and who do they work for?" Red thought to himself.

The chopper began flying away from the area, and did not return. Red and Asadi cautiously ran to the site where the figure had fallen from the helicopter. The position of the victim's head indicated death had been instantaneous upon hitting the ground, snapping his neck. And the number of bullets in his body clearly indicated this was overkill.

Red ran back to the office to check on the people he had sent inside to keep them safe.

"It's Red. Open the door! You are all safe now."

Lily cautiously opened the door and was hysterical. Red naturally assumed the stress had caught up to her, and she was releasing her grief from the realization that her husband was dead. As Red entered the office, Lily pointed to one of the EMTs laying lifeless on the floor. One of the many bullets coming from the helicopter must have sliced through the wall where this young girl had been hiding.

"She had her whole life ahead of her. I am friends with her parents, and they will be completely devastated. What the hell is going on around here Red? Who are these killers invading our town?" Lily passionately asked as she continued sobbing.

Red was right; Lily was grieving, but not for her husband. She was upset at the sudden death of this young girl, but not her husband's death! Red's small police force now had three murders on their hands. Murders at the hands of professional assassins, making Red's job even more difficult.

CHAPTER 6

The next morning brought breaking news of the three murders to the people of this formerly sleepy little town. The Crenna household was shocked by their father's death, but not as upset as most families would be with such a tragic loss of a parent. The Crenna children were more worried about their mother and their futures, as opposed to the loss of their father. Already Lily and Abigail were fighting about Abigail leaving for college. Abigail was insistent on staying home to help her mother and brother with the family logging business, and other household matters.

"Abigail, I appreciate you wanting to help, but it's not necessary. Randy and I can handle things here. You need to get to college and start your future. Please honey, let's not argue about this. I promise to call if we are in need of your help," Lily explained to her daughter.

"How can I possibly go to college knowing what's happened here? I can postpone my college start to the second semester as long as everything is going alright here. With everything that is now on your shoulders, I need to be sure you are ok before I leave," Abigail replied.

Just then Lily's phone rang, "Hi Randy, are you ok?"

"I am fine Mom. I think you and I should meet with the company's executives as soon as possible. We need to be sure they hold the course without Dad being here. You and I also need to discuss the new hierarchy within the organization. Will you take the reins, or will I?" Randy inquired in a much defined, uncaring, monotone voice.

"There is really no question as to who will take over, Randy. Paul wanted you to run the company and that's what will happen. I do agree about the meetings and will meet you at the office later," explained Lily.

Lily agreed to allow Abigail to take a gap year. Abigail's nursing career would still happen, but would begin a year later than expected.

Before going to the logging office, Randy had to set things straight with the hacker group working to take control of the entire government computer system. With Paul now dead, Randy would take over, and the project would now be run his way.

When Randy arrived at the computer repair shop, Boris and Svetlana were already there waiting for him, and they were aware Paul was dead. There were no traditional sympathetic statements from either Boris or Svetlana. They simply got right down to the business at hand.

"With my father dead, the project will continue with me at the helm. Do either of you have a problem with this?" Randy asked in a demanding tone.

Neither Boris nor Svetlana had anything to say because they both knew Randy was not stable.

"So what updates do you two have for me?" continued Randy in an aggressive manner.

"I just made an announcement on prime time television last evening. We announced our administration will mandate that all nonprofit organizations must be vaccinated. This means all employees, volunteers, church members, priests, ministers, and anyone working in any capacity with a nonprofit organization must be vaccinated. Any of these organizations that do not comply with this mandate will lose their nonprofit status with the IRS. They all stand to lose quite a bit of money if they do not comply. This mandate is already monopolizing the news cycle and the backlash from these organizations is fierce. This has had the desired impact of adding to the already strained atmosphere in America," Svetlana explained.

"We still do not have a resolution, or workaround, for our 'start up' glitch. When our system marries with their system, there will be a hiccup, or blinking, which may be noticed by someone," stated Boris.

"My dad said you were the best of the best, which I now know is pure bullshit. I sat in those meetings and listened to you spew your crap day after day. My father trusted you to a fault. Here," Randy thrust a laptop computer to Boris, and continued berating him.

"This is a laptop used by a mid-level government employee. Your job is to code it for concealment of recognition when we log in. You must also unlock the password to allow us to log into the government's system. Once these things are accomplished, you will be able to merge our programming with their operating flow without this ridiculous hiccup you keep referencing. That was real difficult. Right, my little genius?"

Randy could see, and feel, Boris boiling as his face reddened with anger. Randy appeared unfazed and unafraid, which could eventually result in his undoing. Boris had been known to kill people for less than the humiliation Randy had just administered.

"Both of you follow me. We are going to have a quick meeting with the programmers, and we must show a unified front."

"One stupid American is dead! One more to go! This little punk has no idea who he is dealing with," Boris thought to himself as he stood, and then followed Randy into the programming room.

"With my father now dead, I will be continuing his dream with the support of Boris and Svetlana. Our timeline stays the same, so we only have a few days until we execute our plan. If anyone is not fully committed to me and the execution of this plan, you should walk away right now," Randy stated to the group.

One traitor stood up, grabbed a few personal items, and began walking out. The man walked past Randy, Svetlana and Boris without word. As he reached for the door knob, Randy slowly turned toward the traitor, pulling a pistol with a silencer from his coat. Randy quickly placed three bullets into the programmers back, and then turned back to the group saying, "Would anyone else like to leave?"

Randy looked at Boris saying, "Get rid of the body, and make damn sure our timeline is met!"

Randy left the repair shop to head over to the logging meeting he and his mother were planning. With his father not around to maintain control, Randy's psychotic nature was shining through. Paul always knew his son had violent tendencies and irrational breakdowns, but he kept this fact from Lily and Abigail. Paul knew Randy would not harm his family, and had felt he could control him in the outside world. This had all been true, until now!

CHAPTER 7

Alannah and Red Kelly had been through some very tough times during their life together. Red came home from the war in Afghanistan riddled with misplaced guilt over the death of members of his squad. He hit rock bottom, drinking himself from reality, and he pushed away any person who tried to help him. Alannah was a warrior in her own right, and would not give up on the man she loved with all her heart. She pulled Red from the depths of hell through sheer determination and love. Red owed his life to this angel, who had given him another chance to live. They were blessed with a beautiful daughter, and now their blessings would continue, because Alannah was pregnant with twin boys. Red would not let anything happen to his family, and with the recent shootout at the logging office, he believed that his family should leave town. Red felt this was the only way he could ensure their safety, but Alannah did not agree.

"Alannah, I have no idea who we are dealing with, but I do know they are professionals and with me being the local Sheriff, I may now be in their sights. I think it would be a good idea if you and Elmear left for awhile. You could stay with Zach and Layla Morrelli until the dust settles."

"I love you for wanting to keep us safe, but we are not leaving. We go where you go, and I will help keep Elmear and you safe if necessary," replied Alannah.

"Then maybe we should all leave. I could not live with myself if something happened to you, Elmear or our unborn babies," explained Red.

"We will not be the reason you run from a fight. You have always gone head on into battle, and this one will be no different. We will handle it together, Red. Let's start now by locking our home and cars, which we have never had to do while living in Crenna. We should also set the house alarm every night and whenever you are gone. This alarm goes right to your phone, and police headquarters. We should also start to keep a few loaded guns around the house. If we are smart and cautious about this situation, we should be fine Red," replied Alannah.

"You are so stubborn, but I love you. Okay, we will go with your plan, but also, we have to be much more vigilant please. Take note of anything out of the ordinary around the property, or anything that happens while we are out. I have to leave now and begin interviewing people who were close to Paul. Lock the house and set the alarm when I leave. You know where the 9mm's and the ammo are, so please load them when I leave. I love you," Red told Alannah as he left the house. Just before locking the door, Red re-entered their home. "Let's go find the pistols together, load them and be sure there are extra loaded magazines. I need to be sure you are prepared before I leave," Red explained. Alannah gave him a loving smile as they located and prepped the weapons around their home. Red also made sure the pistol that Alannah carried in her purse, was ready for use. Satisfied, Red left the house and Alannah set the alarm once he was gone.

Asadi was at the Southern logging office crime scene, scouring the area for evidence. He did find a bullet lodged in one of the logs near Paul's body, but he did not want to dig the bullet out for fear of damaging the barrel markings. He had the log cut on either side of the bullet hole, and took the entire piece for evidence. Asadi walked in the direction he had theorized the bullet was fired from, and found three shell casings in a thick brush patch on the edge of another log pile. Also, in this thicket was a large damp spot which Asadi thought might have been urine. He put the saturated plants, and shell casings in evidence bags hoping the crime lab would find them useful. Asadi moved from the thicket and continued searching around the nearby log pile. As he walked behind the pile, he took note of the locked safety chain that was missing on the logs that had killed Paul. As he started rounding the corner, Asadi also noted a long pointed piece of wood protruding from one of the lower logs on the large stack. This would have easily sliced Asadi's leg had he not seen it first. He took a closer look at the piece of wood and noticed that in fact it had cut someone's leg. The piece of wood was covered in blood. Asadi carefully cut the bloodied piece of wood from the log and bagged it as another key piece of evidence.

After the previous night's battle, they found that the dead man who had fallen from the helicopter had no identification on him. Red and Asadi were not surprised. The external coroner and crime lab they utilized would take fingerprints, but Asadi knew this man's identity would not easily be revealed, if revealed at all. Asadi moved to the area where they found the dead man and his weapon. He found shell casings all around the area, which he surmised probably came from the AK12-Silencer weapon they had found. These casings were also bagged for the crime lab's analysis.

Once he had scoured the entire office scene, Asadi decided to travel back down the logging roads to search for more evidence. He had no idea what to expect because he had been forced to leave the scene under fire, and did not really take note of its condition. When he arrived at the site where he had left the Sheriff's vehicle, Asadi was surprised that he had made it out safely. The foliage lay broken everywhere from gunfire. The car was riddled with bullet holes, and all the windows were shattered. As he walked the area, Asadi noted there were animal casualties who were caught by surprise and could not escape the slaughter. He was able to find both bullets and casings everywhere, and placed them in his evidence bags. Asadi suspected that the shells and casings found at this scene were from the same weapon that they had found near the dead man that had fallen from the helicopter.

Feeling like he had made a thorough investigation of the area, Asadi called Red to see what he recommended was the next step.

"Hi Red, I am finished here. Where should I take the evidence, and how do we get it there?"

"We need to get it to the crime lab as soon as possible. I have my concerns about getting it to the lab safely. Whoever we are dealing with, may stop at nothing to prevent this evidence from leaving our town. For now, stay where you are. Let me finish speaking with the logging foreman. I want to verify that the EMT was hit by a stray bullet that night. I need to be sure that nothing else happened in the office while they were in hiding. When I finish, I will come see you, and we will make sure you and the evidence make it to our headquarters safely," replied Red.

"10-4. I will see you soon," Asadi responded.

After listening to Red's concerns, Asadi decided he would not wait in the car, but rather would watch the car from a good vantage point where he could not be seen.

The logging foreman could not confirm that the EMT's death was from a stray bullet. His statement given to Red further deepened the mysteries of the previous night's battle.

"After you made sure we were all in the office, we went into hiding, taking cover as you instructed. It was dark, and all I can tell you is at some point during all the commotion, a gun was fired inside that office. I can't tell you who fired the gun, or who might have been hit by the bullet. Right after the gunshot, I did see a figure stand and move towards the back door. Soon after that, I heard a door open and shut. That's all I can tell you. As I said, it was too dark to see anything too clearly," explained the foreman.

"Can you tell me if the figure was male or female, and maybe how tall they were?" asked Red.

"Unfortunately, no I can't. As I said, it was too dark. I can't tell you how tall because they were somewhat crouched and then disappeared," the foreman replied.

"Thanks, that was very helpful information. Please call our office if you remember anything else. We will be in touch if we have any more questions," replied Red as he stood to leave.

Red got into his car and headed out to the Southern logging office to meet Asadi. They needed to get the evidence to a safe spot so Red could figure out how to safely transport it to the crime lab.

The drive to and from the Southern logging office was uneventful. When Red and Asadi returned to the Sheriff's headquarters, they placed all the evidence in the office safe. Red made plans to get it to the crime lab as soon as possible.

CHAPTER 8

"I am so very sorry for your loss. She was not only your EMT partner, she was your friend. I realize that this is not a good time to be asking questions, but it's something I need to do while the incident is fresh in your mind. Can you tell me what happened inside the office after I left you?" Red was getting the second EMT's version of what he saw or heard that night in the logging office.

"After you left, we all took cover wherever we could, and the shooting began. I heard gunshots everywhere, but one shot in particular stood out to me. It sounded like that gunshot came from inside the office. If one of the gunshots did come from inside, I still have no idea if it was the bullet that hit my partner," the EMT explained.

"Thanks very much! I am sorry for the loss of your friend. If you think of anything else, please give me a call," answered Red.

"I know you are just doing your job, Red. I will do whatever I can to help find the person who shot my partner," replied the EMT.

Red felt this second witness brought some consistency to the story that a gun went off inside the office. The dark figure the foreman spoke of was not mentioned by the EMT. Red wondered if this figure could be the same person Lily saw entering the woods. Maybe they circled around the area and went to hide in the office before Red put the people in there for safekeeping. The only one left to talk to was Lily Crenna. Red hoped her story would be similar to the other two witnesses. Before tracking her down for an interview session, Red had to concentrate on getting their evidence to the crime lab.

Red called Asadi to prepare to move the precious cargo.

"Asadi, I think I am being overly cautious, and over thinking how to get the evidence out of town. Please pull everything out, and I will be over soon to pick up you and the evidence. We will drive it to the lab ourselves. The backup car you are using is in no shape for the trip, so we will take mine. I will be there in about five minutes."

Asadi collected everything from the safe and was outside ready to go when Red arrived. The two men loaded the car and were quickly on their way. Red called Alannah to tell her they would return in about two hours. He also contacted the lab, alerting them of their estimated arrival time. It was not only his concern that someone might try to prevent them from reaching the lab, but Red was also concerned about leaving town for a few hours.

The trip was successful, and they arrived back in Crenna without incident. Red notified Alannah of his return, and that he was now going to interview Lily Crenna. This constant communication between the couple was not normal, but was necessary until this case was solved.

Randy and his mother Lily had just started the meeting with the logging company's top level executives. Lily spoke first.

"My husband would want his family's business to continue on as usual. As many of you know, he had been grooming Randy to someday take over control of the company. While it's much sooner than any of us expected, that day has arrived. Randy will immediately take over as head of the company keeping the family's legacy alive."

Suddenly a male voice boomed, "The Crenna's family legacy is not the most pressing issue on the table. A more pressing issue is keeping this business running, thus keeping your town alive and well. Mine is an unfavorable position, but I question your son's ability to handle the current world problems directly impacting the company. I have seen your son in action, and he is neither calm, nor rational in situations that require both. Decisions made by irrational emotions, or any emotion at all for that matter, are more often than not, bad decisions."

    This boisterous gentleman had flown in from across the country to attend this very important meeting. Recently, he had invested a large sum of money in the logging company. This cash infusion had been sorely needed to keep the logging business running. In the short time this man had been associated with the company, he was always at odds with Randy's father, Paul. His interest and conflict with Paul was not all business; there was a personal aspect to his contentious behavior. Randy and Lily were both well aware of this personal situation. Doctor Svetlana Vladmelov was this man's wife.

    Ivan Vladmelov was the third richest man in the world. He owned everything from oil fields to diamond mines to banks, and much, much more. The money invested in this small logging company was meaningless to him, but the personal stake was not. Ivan had many personality traits that he carried on his sleeve. By far, the two traits known to everyone were his ruthlessness and his jealousy. Svetlana is a gorgeous member of the opposite sex, and she used this to her advantage. Married to Ivan, she could have anything she wanted in this world, except one. She enjoyed using her beauty to encourage lust and desire. Svetlana would satisfy a man's lust and desire, get tired of her male victims, then move on to the next. This was why she liked her position with the government: it allowed her to travel and meet men everywhere.

Ivan knew his wife was a player and had caught Svetlana straying from him in the past. She had him so whipped; Ivan would never do anything to harm her. He had no qualms about harming the men she brought into her web. They would quarrel, she would fulfill his desire, and all would be calm until the next time. Well, Paul was the next time!

Ivan, Randy and Lily were all aware of Paul's extracurricular activities, yet each did not know that the other was aware. It was not the logging company that Ivan cared about; it was ruining the Crenna legacy, all the wealth it had created, and the town that carried their name. Randy knew this man was not one to cross with all his connections and ruthless nature. He knew this, but was not going to run from a fight. By whatever means necessary, Randy would keep this company running, and fulfill his father's wishes for the logging company, and the breakdown of America.

CHAPTER 9

Lily had finished the contentious executive meeting. She was headed out for some lunch before she had to meet with her son Randy to discuss what had just taken place in the executive meeting. As she was about to exit the building, Lily saw Red heading inside.

"Hi Red. What brings you here," Lily asked.

"You do Lily. I was hoping to take a few minutes of your time to discuss the night that Paul died. I realize you must have a lot of things going on, but it's important we talk while the night's events remain vivid in your mind," Red explained.

"Can we do this over lunch? I have not eaten in awhile, and I just finished a meeting with terrible results, and have yet another meeting to go to. Actually, along with food I could also use a nice stiff drink," replied Lily.

"As long as we have some privacy to talk, lunch will be fine. Actually, food sounds good, but the drink will have to wait. There are only a few restaurants left in town, so which one do you want to go to?" Red asked.

"Let's go to the bar restaurant that is right up the street. It's close and quick, because I have another meeting to attend, as I said earlier," Lily responded.

They headed to the restaurant which was very empty for it being lunch time. The two were seated in a corner area where they could talk in private. They ordered lunch, one stiff whiskey mule, and then got down to business.

"Can you tell me what happened after I left everyone in the office that night hoping you would all safe?" asked Red.

"There is really not much to tell. Everyone scattered trying to find a safe hiding place. As for me, I knew the layout of the office and went directly to Paul's oak desk and hid underneath it, pulling the desk chair in after me. Then the shooting started outside. Quite frankly, I was shocked that the office was not riddled with several bullets. To think one bullet hit the wall behind Paul's desk, stayed on a path through the door and killed that young girl is, well, to say the least, hard to believe or a really freak accident," Lily explained.

"How do you know a bullet entered the wall behind the desk," Red asked.

"I heard it go through the wall, and then through the wall clock that hung behind Paul's desk. The clock did not fall but the glass shattered as the bullet passed through it. The clock still hangs on the wall, void of glass, and a bullet hole in the center of it," replied Lily.

They quickly finished their meal and Red picked up the bill for lunch.

"Thanks for taking the time to speak with me. I know this is a tough time for you, and your children. Please give me a call if you think of anything else," Red said as they got up to leave.

"Thanks for lunch Red. If I can do anything else, let me know. I have to get to my meeting because I am running late," Lily replied as she quickly headed back toward the logging executive offices.

Red left the restaurant, and headed to the Southern logging office to check out this second bullet story and its trajectory. Red arrived at the office, grabbed his flashlight and went inside the building. Because there had been a report of a gun being fired inside this office, Red wanted to look for a bullet casing. Finding a casing inside the office would corroborate this information. Red first went to Paul's desk, and he immediately noticed the clock hanging on the wall. It was just as Lily described. The clock was hanging on the wall with a bullet hole through the clock face. Following the probable path of this bullet, Red walked to the door frame of Paul's inner office. Lily was very accurate with her description, except the bullet stopped before leaving Paul Crenna's office. This was not the bullet that killed the EMT. This was the second bullet found inside the office that would hopefully help provide some clarity. Analyzing both bullets would indicate the type of gun the two bullets came from. It could help confirm a pistol was fired from inside the office, as suspected by the logging foreman and the second EMT.

The first bullet found in the office was the one that killed the EMT, and Red knew this before talking to Lily. This bullet was part of the evidence they had recently delivered to the crime lab. Red must now get this second bullet to the lab as soon as possible. After digging out the piece of wood housing the bullet, Red began searching the building for a shell casing. As he moved the flashlight to and fro, an object glistened. He walked to the area behind a large chair that was lying on its side. There it was, a shiny shell casing! Red bagged and tagged the evidence, and headed back to the Sheriff's department while calling Asadi on the way.

"Asadi, I have found additional items we need to get to the crime lab. Can you run them over in my car? I still have things to do in town," Red asked.

"Sure Red. I will be outside waiting. There is nothing much going on around here right now anyway."

Asadi's trip to the lab and back was uneventful. Now the painful wait for lab results would begin. Red still wanted to interview Randy and Abigail about their father. In particular, ask them if they knew anyone who might have wanted their father dead.

CHAPTER 10

Lily met Randy in the executive office where her husband Paul had overseen the logging business operations prior to his death. When Lily entered Paul's office, a very eerie feeling came over her. She had spent years of her life with this man, raised a family with him, yet this office was strange to her. She rarely visited, and for that matter he rarely invited her to visit him in this office.

"I had never met Ivan before today, but your father did speak of him from time to time, and it was always with disdain. Why would Paul bring such a nasty individual into our family's business?" Lily asked Randy.

"It definitely was not one of Dad's proudest moments. Ivan can be a charmer, so I really don't know if Dad knew the real Ivan before allowing him to invest in our business. Honestly, lately I got the distinct feeling Dad knew he had made a mistake and was trying to find a way to oust Ivan from the business, and our town. I plan to work with a few of our best people, people we can trust, to find a way to cut Ivan out of our business. This may get messy, so let me handle it," suggested Randy.

"I really want nothing to do with the business. My only concerns are for my children, their security, and the financial security of all the people in this town. This town will be decimated if Crenna logging goes under," replied Lily.

"I will handle this Mom, and if something comes up that you could help with, I will let you know. I have another off-site meeting to get to, so we will talk later," Randy stated.

Lily left to go to the deceased EMT's parents' house to express her condolences to the family. This family had been a casualty of the town's decline. They had to close their hardware store, and now they had lost their only child. Lily felt these good people deserved better, as did many people in this dying town. She was very conflicted, because her heart bled for the people of this town, but on the other hand she really could not care less about the Crenna logging business which the town's people depended on.

Randy's off-site meeting was at the computer repair shop, making sure the launch of his father's plan was executed. Randy pulled into the parking lot and noticed an unknown luxury SUV in his usual executive parking spot. The license plates were from out of state, which created concern, because no strangers should have been allowed into the building. It was the little things that really pissed Randy off, and he stormed into the back of the building yelling, "Who is the idiot who took my parking place?"

A voice coming from the front office yelled, "I did, little boy!"

Randy bolted towards the office, only to stop short when he saw who was inside.

"Well hello. Are you surprised to see me?"

There sat Ivan Vladmelov smiling in all his glory. His wife Svetlana stood by his side, her hand stroking his shoulder with a very coy, but evil grin on her face. She bent down kissing Ivan on the cheek while never taking her eyes off Randy. This evil woman's eyes bore right through Randy psyche, which actually made him shudder. She had played Randy's father, and maybe did so with her husband's approval, which helped Ivan get more control of the logging company.

"Boris, Svetlana, what's going on here? Why would you let him into this area?" asked Randy.

"Boris my friend, if you don't mind, I will answer these questions," Ivan stated calmly.

"Who do you think helped your father fund this operation? Your father had money, and your father used large sums of his money, but it was not enough to fund his failing business, his home and this expensive venture of revenge. So like a super hero, I swooped in to rescue him. Really, you should drop the attitude and thank me for helping."

"I am not my father, I am not your friend, and you can take your money and leave town as soon as possible. We can make it without your money, and without you," shouted Randy.

"Are you done with your tantrum, you cocky, little shit? I am not going anywhere. If you are not careful, you will end up like your father. And for the record, you are not in charge. Boris, you are now in charge of this operation. Randy, you will help Boris see this operation through to the end, or your mother will die. If that fact still does not convince you that I am in charge, then consider your sister will also die if anything goes wrong. I'm not going to let some young, backwoods punk ruin everything that's about to happen. Now junior, have we come to an understanding?" asked Ivan.

Randy knew then he had no choice in the matter. His father had put the entire family at risk because of his blind, uncontrollable revenge towards the American government that he had believed was ruining American lives. Randy just wanted to shoot all three of them right where they sat. At that very moment, Randy felt Ivan may have killed his father. Ivan had multiple reasons. First, there had been his father's affair with Svetlana. Next, his father could have been too vocal about having second thoughts regarding his decision to let Ivan into the family business. Or maybe it was simply Ivan's lack of confidence in Paul's ability to carry out his plan against America. Whatever the reason, Randy felt it was probably Ivan who ordered his father death. This battle was not over in Randy's mind, but for now he would have to submit to Ivan's demands.

"How close are we to executing the plan, and what can I do to help?" asked Randy.

"You can finish the startup protocol you said was easy to program. This is the last piece of programming required. Once completed, we are ready to connect with the government computer system, and start creating havoc, and bringing chaos to the American way of life. The government computer you left me is right there on the table. We need it done by morning," Boris happily ordered Randy.

It was obvious that the town of Crenna had more murders in its future. The big questions were when would they occur, who would the next victims be, and who would do the murdering?

CHAPTER 11

"Abigail, why are you limping? Did you hurt your leg or foot somehow?" Lily wondered watching her daughter come into the house.

"I'm fine mom. I just had one hell of a workout at the gym, and every muscle in my body hurts. I have been getting soft lately, and decided I had to finally do something about it. I think I put a year's worth of workouts into a single, two-hour session. I went way overboard for my first workout, and I am now paying the price. I just want to go soak the pain away in a hot tub for hours," explained Abigail.

Before Lily could respond to Abigail, the doorbell rang and she went to see who it was. Lily carefully cracked the door without removing the safety chain lock. Once she saw it was Red, Lily unchained the lock and opened the door.

"Hi Red. Wow! I get to see you twice in one day, which is more than I see you in a normal week. Come in," Lily chuckled and let him in. "So what can I do for you this time," Lily asked as she closed the door behind him.

"I am actually here to see your daughter Abigail, if it's ok with the two of you. I just have a few questions," explained Red.

"I don't understand why you would need to question her! Abigail was nowhere near the area of her father's murder. Is there something else going on that I should know about?" Lily asked.

"I realize Abigail was not there. I am just trying to find out if people close to Paul knew of anyone who might hate him enough to kill him," Red replied.

Abigail was nearby and heard Red's question. She was more than happy to answer his question and any more he might have.

"Mom, I can handle this. It's okay with me, but are you absolutely sure that you want to hear what I have to say?" Abigail asked her mother.

"Sorry. It's the mom in me trying to protect the young ones that are really not so young anymore. If you are okay with me being here, then yes, I want to hear everything you have to say," replied Lily quietly.

"I can think of quite a few people who disliked the man you call my father. But, the reality is, I have no way of knowing if those same people wanted him dead. You can start with his many trollops, and some of their husbands from around town. He went from woman to woman; so you have jealousy, and possibly their husband's jealousy, as motives. I mean let's start with Svetlana. The entire town had known they were rendezvousing. Now, add her powerful husband Ivan into the equation, who had to know this was going on, and this equals hatred and anger. Then, how about the young EMT, who just died at his murder scene. How ironic is that? Yes Mom, the very girl you cried over was boffing your husband. Maybe her parents knew and they were upset at 'Pauly the Casanova of Crenna, Maine'," Abigail ranted with indignation.

Lily was quite emotional, which seemed very odd to Red, based on the fact that her husband had just died and she had not shed a single tear over his death. Red thought maybe the tears were embarrassment, over the reality that her daughter had known all those sordid details about her father. He also considered that maybe they were tears of anger over how Paul had decimated their family, and their long standing reputation in the area. The town of Crenna was not the only thing crumbling; the very founders' family name and reputation were dying as well. Red did not want to upset Lily more, so he asked if Abigail would come down to the Sheriff's department and make a statement. At headquarters, Paul or Asadi would interview each woman, husband or parent who might be involved with Paul's sordid lifestyle. From this list of names they would begin their investigation into possible suspects to try to find a motive. Abigail agreed to stop by later, so Paul thanked the two women and turned to leave the house when Lily stopped him.

"Red, there is one name that strikes a chord with me. Earlier today Randy and I had a meeting with the logging company's upper level executives. As crazy as it sounds, I was aware of Paul's indiscretions with Svetlana Vladmelov. What I did not know was that her husband had a major financial interest in the logging company. Ivan Vladmelov was at today's meeting and made no bones about him not being in favor of Randy running the company. The man is rude, very direct, and gave me a very uncomfortable feeling. I know this may be a ridiculous statement, but I left the meeting feeling Ivan was capable of very dangerous things to protect his wife, and their financial interests," Lily explained.

"Thank you so much for your frankness and honesty, Abigail and Lily. Abigail, please come down to the office as soon as you can, and if I am not there, Asadi will handle your statement. I will keep you posted Lily," Red stated as he walked out the door shaking his head.

Red was headed to the computer repair shop to see if Randy was there. If he did not find him, then Red would go to the executive offices of the Crenna logging company. He was intrigued with both Abigail and Lily's comments, but was most focused on Lily's statements about Ivan and Svetlana. Red knew of both of these people, because they had recently purchased one of the larger homes in the area. Red had just assumed it was a vacation home because the town rumor mill touted the vast amounts of financial resources the Vladmelovs had acquired over the years. They did not seem like the type of people to settle down in such a small town which brought Red to his vacation home theory.

It was not long before Red arrived at the repair shop. He went inside and asked the counter person if Randy was around, and if so, did he have time to speak with Red. She picked up the phone, apparently to call Randy's office to check on his status. "He will be up in just a few moments," she informed Red after hanging up the phone. It did not take long for Randy to come through the door leading to the office area.

"Hi Red, what can I do for you? Is the department having computer problems again?" asked Randy.

"No, we didn't mess up our computer again. I wanted to discuss your father's murder with you. Can we go into your office, or another private area in the building?" asked Red.

Randy quickly agreed and walked Red into the back where the offices were located. Randy was in the lead and opened the door behind the counter. They entered an area of the repair shop that Red had never been in before. To the left was what looked like a conference room, and to the right was probably Randy's office. Red was just about through the door when he noticed Ivan and another male sitting in the conference room.

Ivan's eyes met Red's, and at the same time Randy realized his mistake and turned around quickly telling Red, "We don't have to leave the front area. I will make the counter person leave, and we will have the entire front area to ourselves."

Red calmly said, "Okay, wherever you are most comfortable," and they both went back to the front counter area. This was a very odd, but telling encounter for Red. When asked, Randy said he had no idea who might be mad enough to kill his father. This was the complete opposite interview than his sister had given. How could Abigail know so much and then Randy act like he knew nothing, Red wondered. What was most intriguing to Red was Ivan's presence at Randy's little computer repair shop. Had Ivan also invested in this business? Red left the building with an unsettled feeling, but knew he had two more interviews to conduct. Ivan and Svetlana were now very much on his radar.

CHAPTER 12

Randy returned to the conference room and sat down. Ivan was standing and moved his face to within inches of Randy's, and proceeded to give him a verbal lashing.

"You are a real moron. Why would you bring anyone into this highly sensitive area of the building, let alone a Sheriff? Are you looking to sabotage the implementation of all our hard work? More importantly, are you looking to get your mother and sister killed? The Sheriff saw me, made eye contact, and more than likely saw Boris as well. There is absolutely no doubt in my mind he left wondering why I would be in the back room of a small, computer repair shop. I cannot believe you were that stupid," Ivan glared, practically spitting, he was so mad.

Randy was not one to be intimidated, but Ivan was masterful in the art of conveying his vitriol, which now filled the room. Now

Randy could only hope that his purposeful mistake would lead to Red questioning Ivan, and not lead to his mother and sister's death.

"Red said nothing about you. He was here asking if I knew of anyone who disliked my father enough to murder him. I told him my father had enemies, but none that I knew who would want him dead," replied Randy.

"You better hope your Sheriff does not start sniffing around about me. Did you finish the program allowing our system to mirror the government system without detection?" asked Ivan.

"Yes, we are ready to go when Boris confirms everything else is ready to go," Randy cautiously informed Ivan.

Ivan swiveled his chair slightly to the right to face Boris, "Boris, are we now completely ready to go?"

"Yes. We are ready," Boris quickly replied.

"Then let's do this. I want constant updates on our progress. Remember, we are doing this my way now, not Paul's," grunted Ivan.

Ivan simplified how they were going to stimulate unrest in American society. Paul had programmed this complicated plan to restructure the flow of money within America. Ivan was simply going to stop the flow of money from the government into the American daily financial system; <u>from</u> the government not <u>to</u> the government!

The American people had been conned into thinking that they lived in a free Republic or Democracy, while in reality neither was true. First of all, these terms were so similar, it made their use in America confusing at best. Ivan believed that neither term could be used as a descriptor to identify America's system of political/government operation. Capitalism, Socialism, Democracy, Dictatorship, Communism, Anarchism, Progressivism, and more were on the list of government descriptors. America was the mutt of the world as it used parts of each of those systems. There was one simple term that captured how to ruin the America economy, and how to cripple America: MONEY! If you turn off the government money spigot, America will crumble, and chaos will surely to follow.

Outside the computer repair building, Red was in the squad car considering his next move. He had left the building with the intention of leaving the area and heading to the Sheriff's department to fill Asadi in on his findings thus far. But, now he wondered if he should go back inside the repair shop to speak with Ivan. He knew

Ivan was in the building, which would prevent Red the hassle of trying to find him in the future. There was also the risk that Ivan could leave town at a moment's notice on business, which meant Red would lose his chance to speak with him. Red decided now was the time, left his car and re-entered the computer repair shop.

"Hi, sorry to bother you again, but I need to speak with Mr. Ivan Vladmelov. I saw him in one of the first two rooms in the back," Red explained to the clerk at the counter.

Ivan was still daydreaming about his new plan that had just been executed. He was startled when he heard the counter clerk tell Randy that Red was in the shop again. Then Ivan heard that Red wanted to meet with him. Randy excused the clerk, telling her he would deliver the message to Ivan. As he walked toward Ivan, Randy could feel the heat emanating from Ivan's rage after he heard the Sheriff wanted to speak with him.

"I can tell him you left," suggested Randy.

"No, you have done enough damage. I will talk to him in your office, so go get him. Boris, go to the back and make sure everything is going as planned. I don't want the Sheriff to see you if he has not already done so," ordered Ivan.

Randy went out front, and upon seeing Red, welcomed him to come into his office. Once in the office, Red sat down and Randy left, shutting the door behind him. Ivan sat stoically behind the desk glaring at Red, who spoke first.

"Mr. Vladmelov, I am Liam Kelly, the local Sheriff. Around town I am known to people as Red Kelly. My department is investigating the murder of Paul Crenna. It has come to my attention that you knew Paul through Crenna logging, in which you have invested some of your vast wealth. I am asking anyone who knew Paul if they would have any idea who might want him dead. Are you aware of any business acquaintances who Paul may have angered?" Red asked Ivan.

Ivan was a calculated, manipulative man who began weaving his story. Just by using his given name Liam, as opposed to his nickname Red, Ivan was making a silent combative statement.

"Liam, it's nice to meet you. I have heard that you are well liked by the townspeople, and that you take very good care of this town. As you know, I am somewhat new to the area and to the company. Yes, I did invest money in Crenna logging, but have tried to allow Paul to run the company, with me providing him only suggestions to better his company's financial status. The only glaring friction I have witnessed was between Randy Crenna and his father Paul. Randy outwardly disapproved of the way his father was running the company, and wanted control before his father bankrupted the company Randy was to take over. Now, I cannot imagine a son killing his father, but you asked about bad business dealings, and this is the only one I have witnessed. It is something you will probably not hear from local executives, because they have been friends with the Crenna family for many years. I look at things without emotion, so take it for what it's worth, Liam. I am trying to assimilate into this nice quiet town. The people are very warm and welcoming, and I love the beautiful lake in the middle of town. I saw you and your family there over the weekend, and I have to tell you that your daughter is so very cute. You should be a very proud daddy. If you have no more questions, I have to get to the airport," explained Ivan.

    The hair on the back of Red's neck stood up as he soaked up the evil emanating from this arrogant little man. Red casually ended the conversation, thanked Ivan for his information and wished him a safe journey. Red intuitively received Ivan's passive-aggressive threat to his own family loud and clear, and he knew the next move was up to him.

CHAPTER 13

The computer merge was going flawlessly. Soon they would have control of the government finances without anyone's knowledge. The government system would continue to look like it was operating normally, when in actuality it would become a useless set of fake transactions.

"Boris, I am leaving Randy in your hands. Since we are just beginning to control the government's finances, I am concerned that if we kill any of his family members right now, it will throw him off his game. If something changes dramatically, you do whatever you need to do to keep this project hidden and moving forward. Also, ready the men, and the helicopter. If the Sheriff's questions lead him anywhere near what's going on in this building, you are to take the steps we discussed in private to keep his department at bay," instructed Ivan.

"Understood, Mr. Vladmelov! As the programs continue to run in tandem, Randy's importance will become less and less. If trouble begins, it might be wise to kill him, and not the family members," replied Boris.

"As I said, you do whatever you think is best to keep everything hidden and on track," instructed Ivan.

Ivan Vladmelov left though the back door, but had no intention of leaving for the airport. He needed a private place to take care of some business dealings over the phone. Unbeknownst to Ivan, as he left the repair shop through the back, his wife Svetlana was entering the building through the front door. As Red was pulling out of the parking lot, he saw Svetlana going into the building. He did a quick U-turn because he also needed to question Svetlana, and more importantly he wondered why she was going into the computer repair shop.

For the third time that day Red got out of his car, and went into Randy's computer repair store.

"Yep, it's me again. I just saw Svetlana Vladmelov come into the building. Please let Randy know I need to speak with her as well. Thank you," Red explained to the counter person.

The clerk went into the back again to let Randy know Red was out front. Randy was showing signs of nerves. He was worried that Ivan's eye and ears, Boris, was still inside the building. Boris watched Randy go to the front, and then return with Red, the new thorn in their side. Randy led Red into the conference room. Boris took a quick detour to call Ivan.

As he walked away, Boris heard Randy say, "She went into the ladies room. I am sure she will be right out."

Red knew Boris was hovering, but had never met the man before, and really wondered what his role was in this little shop. His thought process was broken when Svetlana entered the room and immediately turned on the charm.

"Now why would a handsome Sheriff like you, want to speak with little old me? Did my Omicron advice on television offend someone?" Svetlana asked as her eyes fluttered at Red.

"This woman is sly, and knows how to handle herself. She is a Southern Belle with a Russian accent," Red thought to himself before responding.

"My name is Liam, Mrs. Vladmelov, and most people call me Red. I am here to discuss Paul Crenna's murder. From what I have been told, you knew Paul quite well, and I am wondering if you have knowledge of anyone who might have wanted to see Mr. Crenna meet an untimely death," asked Red.

All of a sudden Ivan came storming into the office. Red really disliked this man, and felt the need to antagonize him further.

"Mr. Vladmelov, I thought you had a plane to catch. Did they cancel your flight?"

"Why are you here harassing my wife? She has had no dealings with Crenna so you should not have any questions to ask her?" Vladmelov bellowed.

"My first concern is, how did you know I was here? Is this office illegally videotaping an officer of the law? I really do not find it necessary to discuss an official investigation with anyone, let alone you, in your current state of agitation. Please leave the room so I may continue or I can take legal steps to have Svetlana come to the Sheriff's department to answer questions. It's your choice. And by the way, your wife did know Paul Crenna," Red replied caustically.

"Honey calm down. It's ok. I did know Paul, and you knew that. You must have forgotten with all the business things you have on your mind. This cute little Sheriff's questions are legitimate so I will just answer them my love," Svetlana explained to her fuming, angry husband, Ivan.

Reluctantly, Ivan left the office. Red noticed something odd as Ivan walked past the big man he had heard called Boris. Ivan looked him in the eyes, nodded his head yes, and kept walking. Upon recognizing this nod, Boris pulled out his phone and walked to a quiet area.

"I did know Paul intimately, and why not? The man's wife hadn't even touched him in years. I know of no one, outside his immediate family, who would have wanted to kill Paul. Have you talked with his conniving wife? She acts all sweet and innocent, but that woman is a bitch in sheep's clothing. How about her son, who wants nothing more than to take over the logging company? Do you have any more questions for me?" asked Svetlana.

"I appreciate your candor Mrs. Vladmelov. I am wondering what all you people are doing in Randy's little computer repair shop. Did your husband invest in this little shop as well?" replied Red.

Red knew he was pushing the limits of his legal questioning, but he also felt something else was going on inside this building.

"Liam, you know that question has nothing to do with your case, but I love that you are so cute," answered Svetlana.

"That was more of a non-official question. It just seems like there are some high powered people here for such a small enterprise. It's my natural curiosity, nothing more. Again, I thank you for your help. If you think of anything else that might be of importance to the case, please give me a call," Red said to Svetlana as he handed her a card with the Sheriff's department's phone number.

Once again, Red left the building and hoped it was for the last time that day.

Across town, three strange men entered Crenna's only remaining car repair shop. This was a father/son-owned business with only the father on site today. One of the men approached the father who was leaning over the engine of a car and asked in very broken English, "Good afternoon. Can you tell me if our Sheriff's car is now fixed and ready for us to pick-up? We could really use it today."

The father stood up from his working position over the engine to see who was asking about the Sheriff car. Not knowing any of these men, adding to the fact that he did not like the looks of these men, the father replied, "I will need to hear from Red or Asadi to release the car to you guys."

One of the men pulled a gun out of his coat pocket, pointed it at the owner and asked about the Sheriff's car one more time.

CHAPTER 14

"Mom, I think it's time some things were brought out into the open. I never said anything before this, because I didn't want to hurt you. Paul was merely a sperm donor to me. He ran around on you with any woman in town that would have him. He completely ruined the name of the very man that built this town, and the family logging empire. While the collapse of the company is not entirely Paul's fault, he made decisions that assisted this collapse rather than fight it. Why would he bring in a Russian madman when there were plenty of other local investors ready to join the logging team?" Abigail emotionally said to her mother.

"I have no idea what Paul's reasoning was for bringing the Vladmelovs into the business and this town. I know you are right about Paul's indiscretions, and I should have left him years ago. I guess I am one of those high-maintenance bitches who have little self esteem, and will not leave the money. Regardless of all these issues, I still would never have wished him dead," replied Lily.

Shockingly, Abigail responded by saying, "Well, I did!"

Abigail left the room, limped upstairs, leaving her mother stunned and in tears. Abigail went into her room, grabbed a change of clothes and went to take a long soothing bath. After undressing, and before getting into the tub, Abigail had to clean her wound. She sat in the vanity chair, and carefully removed the blood-soaked gauze that was wrapped around the deep gash in the lower part of her leg. She placed the soiled gauze into the toilet, flushing it a few times so it did not clog, and to make sure all the evidence disappeared. Abigail laid her leg over the tub, and poured hydrogen peroxide all over the wound so the excess blood would go down the drain. No one would know of this wound to her leg. She rinsed the tub, and then filled it with clean warm water, climbing in to soak, relax and think. Abigail knew her predicament was far from over, but for now she needed to keep playing the blame game, which would hopefully keep any focus off her. She would not lose what was rightfully hers, so if it meant her brother Randy had to take the fall, then so be it.

Randy was having his own set of issues when Boris entered his office with the look of death, Randy's death, all over his ugly face.

"You have jeopardized everything that you and your father have worked so hard to accomplish. We have your mother, and sister under constant surveillance. The next mistake, or visit from the Sheriff, I will give the okay, and one of them will be dead in seconds. Do you understand?"

"You really are an idiot. Ivan made things perfectly clear, but you knew that. You just had to flex your fake muscles, didn't you Borass," Randy replied with arrogance.

In an instant Boris reared his right arm back. With the force of an ex-boxer his fist flew forward squarely onto Randy's jaw. Randy's entire body flew backwards bouncing off the wall and onto the floor.

Boris shook his hand in pain saying, "I guess that's fake blood from my fake fist that hit you! You are such an idiot; you are leading your entire family to death. Get up, clean off your face and get me an update for Ivan."

Lily started getting the house secured so they could go to bed. Windows shut, blinds closed, doors locked, alarm set, all the things she never felt she had to do before, until now. As Lily was pulling one of the front blinds down, she caught a glimpse of something outside. She noticed strange men when one of them took a deep draw on their cigarette, creating a glow at the end of the stick. This glow on such a dark night lit an area large enough for Lily to see a few people milling around outside their driveway's iron gate. Lily quickly grabbed her cell phone to call Red.

"Hi Lily, this is Alannah. Hang on a minute, Red is in the kitchen."

"Alannah, please hurry I have strange men outside watching my home."

"Lily, its Red, and I heard you. Get into hiding upstairs, and keep your cell phone with you. I am on the way," Red said.

Red reminded Alannah to lock and alarm the house, and then he flew out the door calling Asadi on the way out.

"Asadi, Lily Crenna has some unknown people apparently watching her home. We need to get out there to see exactly what these people are doing. Please come up to her home from the South end of the street. I am coming in from the North side to be sure none of them leave."

"Understood Red, I am on the way to my car now. Be safe and I will see you there," Asadi replied as he jumped into his car.

Lily ran upstairs as Red instructed. She knocked on the bathroom door waking Abigail from a relaxing nap in the tub.

"Abigail, get dressed now. There are people outside watching our house. I have called Red and he is on the way."

Abigail jumped out of the tub, dried herself and put on an old sweat suit to cover herself and her wound. She came out of the bathroom, and Lily led her to the master bath on the far side of the house.

"How do you know they are watching our house? Maybe you are just a little paranoid with everything going on around town?" whispered Abigail.

"Maybe, but I am not taking any chances right now," replied Lily.

Red and Asadi arrived in perfect sequence, driving towards the house from opposite directions. Red's headlights showed three people leaning against the stone structure that held one side of the large wrought iron gate at the entrance of the Crenna driveway. From the other direction, Asadi placed his headlights on the parked car making sure there was no one inside. Both men got out of their cars and walked toward the three unknown people.

"Are you here waiting for someone? Did your car break down, and if so can I call a tow truck for you or take you somewhere?" Red asked the strangers.

"We were just enjoying the beautiful evening. Is that a crime in this backwoods hick town?" one of the men asked, with the other two chuckling sarcastically as they swaggered around the area. The stranger's accent was clearly Russian, which immediately brought thoughts of the Vladmelovs to Red's mind.

"Actually, if one of you brilliant trespassers would read the sign on the end of this stone structure, it will tell you why in fact you are breaking the law," Red informed the trio.

The speaker of the group turned and looked at the sign, but said nothing. He turned back at Red and just stared at him aggressively.

"Well, because we are a friendly town, I will read it for you. The sign shows two very simple words, 'NO TRESPASSING.' In

America, that means if you ignore the sign, you are in fact breaking the law. Turn around and put your hands on the stone," Red informed the strangers.

By now Asadi had drawn his gun and had it pointed at the three men. One by one, Red zip tied their hands, and escorted two of them into his car, and the third into Asadi's car. Normally, they would not have reacted like this, but with the recent strange happenings in the area, to be safe Red felt he had to take these people in for questioning.

Red stepped aside and called Lily to let her know what had transpired. He wanted to let her know she was safe, at least for now. Red and Asadi left the area with their three prisoners. When they arrived at the Sheriff's department, the three strangers were locked inside the only jail cell in Crenna.

CHAPTER 15

Red and Asadi stayed on duty the entire night. Red kept an eye on the Crenna house to be sure there were no more unwanted visitors. Asadi stayed at the Sheriff's office to keep an eye on their three guests living in their jail "bed and breakfast." When morning came, Red checked in with Lily to be sure she and Abigail were alright. While they were doing fine that moment, both were worried what might happen to them when Red left the area. This was also a concern of Red's, but he knew he could not guard them 24/7, so the best thing he could do was to try to get to the bottom of what was happening around their town.

Red headed to his home for a few hours of much needed sleep. When he got home Alannah was carefully locking their baby Elmear into her car seat. Red had forgotten that today was Alannah's doctor's appointment with the obstetrician.

"Hold on baby. Let me just do a quick change, and I will be right out to go with you," Red said to his wife.

"Red, it's alright honey. This is just a routine checkup that I can handle. You need to get in there and get some sleep. Are Lily and Abigail alright?" Alannah asked.

"They are fine, at least for today. Are you sure about going to this appointment without me?" Red replied.

"We will be fine Red. We are only going to the doctor's office, and will be back within a few hours, so please get inside and get some sleep. We will both see you later my love," answered Alannah as she got into her car. Red ran around the car to give Elmear a kiss and a hug, and then ran back around to the driver's side to give Alannah a kiss.

"You are carrying a weapon, correct?" asked Red.

"Absolutely. Now get in there and get some sleep!" Alannah replied lovingly.

Red gave her another kiss, and the two most important people in his life drove away. Red watched them until their car was out of sight, and then went inside to try to get a few hours of sleep. Sleep did not come easy, because Red felt he should not have let his wife go alone. He could not get these thoughts out of his head, and tossed and turned for some time.

With a gun pointed at him, the owner of the car repair shop had no choice but to show the intruders where the squad car was located. He led them to the office, and opened a key box filled with hanging keys. He pulled out a set of keys, began walking out the back door of the building, and was dead the minute the strangers got sight of the squad car. The three foreign looking killers quickly got into the Sheriff's squad car and left the area. Two of the three men ducked out of view in the back seat of the car.

There was only one main road in and out of Crenna, which made things easy for the assailants. The thugs knew what car to look for, so they parked on the side of the main road miles away from town. They made it look like the Sheriff's squad car was set up to do radar speed checks along the road. The person commanding these mercenaries did not want them to handle this delicate task by directly attacking the house, creating more immediate visibility to the mission. Through their paid informant network, the group was told their target would be on this road today. When the victim's vehicle drove past the squad car, they would complete the mission in a more private setting that would be less visible for a period of time. This would also give the men a longer escape window. If this plan did not take shape, they would have to take action at the home of the victims.

Alannah was singing an Irish children's song to Elmear while driving through town. As she drove the streets of this quaint, little town, her song was silenced by her sudden, sad thoughts that Elmear may not be able to grow up in this idyllic American town. If the town continued on its death spiral, they would eventually be forced to move. Elmear was sleeping when Alannah steered the car onto the main road. After leaving town, the roadside views changed from beautiful old buildings to the beauty of woods, fields and nature. There was the occasional house or farm and even a few dirt roads leading to places unknown. The shadows of branches from majestic trees, lined the road in front of her. It was a beautiful sunny day to take a drive on such a scenic route through the mountains.

Just after passing one of the mountain dirt roads, Alannah heard the sounds of a siren. She glanced in her rear view mirror and smiled at the sight of the oncoming Sheriff's car. Since Red was home in bed it had to be Asadi playing games. Asadi was a gently, fun loving man who Alannah wished had someone to love. He was a dear friend whose loyalty was never ending. Alannah played the game, put her turn signal on, and pulled over to the side of the road and turned the car's engine off.

Watching in her door's side mirror, the moment the man exited the squad car Alannah knew it was not Asadi. The two other men in the back seat popped up, and exited the squad car. She considered starting her car to speed away, but the sight of the guns caused her to re-consider and take another defensive action.

Alannah calmly grabbed the pistol that was holstered to her driver's side door. She carefully moved it under her coat and pointed it towards the passenger side door. Then she removed a second gun from her purse lying in the seat next to her. With this second gun in her hand she formed an 'X' by crossing over her other hand pointing this second gun towards the driver side door.

The driver of the squad car walked to the driver side front window. A second man walked to the passenger side, front window. The third assailant hung back, apparently in a support position. In a very aggressive move, the man at Alannah's window used the butt of his gun to tap on the window. This tactic was obviously to inform

Alannah all these men were armed, which would have terrified most people in this deadly situation.

Muffled, because her window remained closed, Alannah could hear the man say, "No one will get hurt if you follow our direction. Please open the door and get out of the car."

Alannah calmly shook her head no, continuing to stare straight ahead using her peripheral vision to watch for any sudden aggressive movements from the two of them. The man at her window asked the same question one more time, and he received the same response from Alannah. After a short waiting period, both men looked at each other, nodded in psychic agreement, and began moving their guns upward into a firing position. Without hesitation Alannah began squeezing the trigger of both guns and did not stop until only one bullet remained in each clip. The two thugs had no chance to fire a single shot as their bodies flew backwards with each bullet. Both men fell to the ground and would never get up again.

Elmear was crying, but was safe for now! Alannah bent down to reach for her phone which flew from her hand as the car suddenly lunged forward. Man number three had run back to the stolen squad car when the gunfire began. When the shooting finally stopped, he used the squad car as a battering ram in hopes of rendering Alannah unconscious, or better yet dead. Elmear would be upset, but unharmed in her well-designed car seat. When Alannah bent to get her cell phone, her head was in a precarious position when the air bag burst. The blow rendered her unconscious, which allowed the kidnapper to complete part of their mission. He got out of his car with his gun drawn, and quickly released Elmear from her car seat. He and the baby returned to the damaged, but functioning, squad car. He placed Elmear into the car's seat belts as best he could for the short drive. The original plan was to take the car seat for the baby, but fear caused this third man to become haphazard, which would not serve him well in the future. When he began to drive the damaged car, steam billowed from the engine compartment, and one of the front tires was making a piercing, grinding noise. He had no choice but to push this wreck to its limits, and hope it had enough life to make it to the final destination.

  The squad car sped back to the dirt road where it had been originally parked along the main road. The frightened man drove miles down the dirt road where he turned right onto yet another dirt road that led deeper into the woods. Just like in the movies, in the middle of the woods a clearing appeared, and waiting there was a helicopter waiting to take off. This was no ordinary helicopter due to its unique construction. It was small in comparison to most, but its small unique design allowed it to be quickly disassembled, and hauled away in an innocuous tractor trailer. The driver stopped the car, removed Elmear, and strapped her into the specially attached car seat inside the helicopter. Within minutes they were airborne, flying low through the fields and power line cutouts. This was a dangerous, but necessary maneuver, which would get them to their destination quickly, and without detection.

    Alannah awoke to complete silence and the realization her baby was gone. She fumbled for her phone to call Red, but to no avail because she passed out again.

CHAPTER 16

Boris had been trying to contact his band of sleuths who were given the task of watching the Crenna home. He had tried every hour on the hour for the last three hours, and failed to make contact. Boris was not worried about their well being, but he was angry they were not answering their phones to provide him with updates. He had made it perfectly clear to the group that they were to be alert, and ready to move on his command via cell phone. Right now the only excuse he would accept for their incompetence was death. If he found them dead, then and only then, would he understand their inability to answer their phone!

"Randy, I have to step out for a little while. Call me if any issues arise," bellowed Boris.

Boris left the repair shop to check and see if his men were still watching the Crenna house as they had been instructed. It also gave him a chance to clear his head from all the challenges he was handling for Ivan. When he reached the area near the Crenna residence, Boris slowed his vehicle, and began carefully checking both sides of the road for signs of his men. He drove by their empty vehicle, and soon realized the three were nowhere in sight. Boris turned the car around, and drove past the Crenna's once again to check for any sign of his men. Still, they were nowhere in sight, so Boris decided to try calling them just one more time.

Asadi was still babysitting the three men they had found trespassing on Crenna's property. Before putting them in the jail cell, each had to empty their belongings into three separate manila envelopes. The past few hours one of these envelopes kept ringing, and Asadi was tired of hearing the noise. He opened the envelope, grabbed the annoying phone, and pushed the answer icon firmly saying, "Sheriff's department, how may I help you?" Asadi heard nothing and the phone call quickly ended.

The moment Boris left the computer repair shop, Randy had gone to the men's room with his cell phone. This was the only room in the building with no camera, or monitoring system.

"Mom, you and Abigail need to leave town now. There are things happening that I cannot tell you about, or that I can control. I have to find a way out of this mess, but until I do, you two must leave town. Go to the family cabin immediately and I will be in touch."

Randy quickly hung up the phone, and went back into the programming area adjusting his pants as if he had just gone to the bathroom.

Lily had been confused by the call, but the recent surveillance of their property gave credence to Randy's request. She had decided she would listen to Randy and leave for their cabin deep in the woods. Abigail did not agree, and would not agree to go with her mother.

"I do not understand why you won't go with me. With what happened last night, and Randy's concern, we need to leave town now for awhile," Lily pleaded with her daughter.

"I am not going anywhere on the advice of my elusive brother. He just wants us out of his hair while he takes complete control of the business. I know you told him it's what Paul wanted, but I want to see the legal documents turning everything over to him. I am not leaving town until I see them. I deserve partial control of this family legacy, and refuse to just walk away without legal proof that it was left to him," replied a very angry Abigail.

Lily would not leave this town without her daughter. The only thing she could think to do was to hire a private security team to guard them and their home until this was over.

After realizing that the Sheriff's office had one of his men's cell phones, Boris left the side of the road and began driving furiously back towards town. He came upon a small bridge that lay over a deep, fast moving creek. Boris slowed, stopped, rolled down the window and tossed his phone into the water. He then pulled a second burner phone from his console, and immediately texted the new phone number to Ivan and a few others. Boris left the area and headed to the computer repair shop. Once there he went inside to assess his next step, now that he knew three of his henchmen were in jail.

As Boris blew through the programming area he demanded that Randy follow him to the office.

"I have to call Ivan in ten minutes with a progress report. Is everything on schedule? Have we stopped payments to the military,

Social Security, government workers, state subsidies, etc?" asked Boris.

"Everything is going as planned. Within the next day or two, people checking their mail and bank account will begin to worry. This worry will soon turn to anger," replied Randy.

Randy left the office, and once again went into the secure bathroom. He pulled his phone out and texted, *"It's time to pull out. We will be at the pickup location at the appointed time."*

CHAPTER 17

A phone call from the crime lab alerting him that the results of the evidence they had submitted was completed woke Red from his much needed, albeit very short nap. Red wanted to remain in town until Alannah returned from her doctor's appointment, so he asked Asadi to once again make the trip to the crime lab to bring the results back to the Sheriff's department. Red would relieve him to be sure their three prisoners were safe and secure. Asadi left immediately when Red arrived at the Sheriff's station. Both men were going on little to no sleep, but both were also adept at coping with little rest from their time in Afghanistan.

Asadi did not feel like traveling the main road out of town today. He decided to take a secondary road that travels deeper through the beautiful mountains with twists and turns that would keep him awake. With his window down, he could see and hear the wind rustling through the many trees along the side of the road. As

Asadi broke the crest of a hill his calm drive was interrupted by a large tractor trailer attempting to pull onto the road from a rundown, dirt road. While he found this highly unusual, it was certainly not illegal. But he felt compelled to stop and see if they needed help. He turned on the squad car's emergency lights and pulled to the side of the road.

Exiting his car Asadi walked to the man standing outside, apparently directing the driver as he was backing into the mouth of the dirt road.

"Are you guys ok; you are off the beaten path with this tractor trailer. This road has seen very few trucks like this unless they were hauling logs," stated Asadi.

"We are fine. Our phone mapping system kept going in and out of service up here in the mountains. As a result we must have taken a wrong turn," the man said in very broken, but understandable English. Asadi's senses heightened because, after hearing the man speak, Asadi felt for sure he was Russian. Again, this was not illegal, but without question it was very odd.

"Where were you headed?" asked Asadi becoming more inquisitive about the situation.

"We are headed to 'X Logistics' to drop off our load. We were just turning around to get headed back in the right direction. We are ok now, and ready to get back on the road. Thanks for stopping to check on us," the man replied in a slightly irritated tone.

Asadi wished them well, got back into his car and continued on his trip. As he passed the front of the truck he waved goodbye while locking a picture of the license plate in his mind. The men gave a cordial wave, and went about their business.

Before leaving the area, the truckers went back to open the trailer doors to be sure the load had not shifted with all the twists and turns they had encountered. They unlocked and opened the two large doors of the trailer. One man jumped into the trailer to be sure things in the front had not shifted. With everything intact, the man jumped off the truck and said, "All parts of the helicopter are secure, and nothing has shifted. We are good to go." They shut and re-locked the trailer doors, jumped back into the truck and were on their way.

"Do you think we should have let that cop go?" the passenger asked the truck driver.

"Yes. He didn't suspect anything. He is a small town, wannabe cop. Shooting him would just create more issues when they found the body," replied the driver.

"Red, I just had an interesting encounter on the mountain road to town," Asadi said to him on his cell phone.

Asadi explained the entire situation, and gave Red the license plate number to run the tag while Asadi remained on the phone.

"The plate number is coming back registered to a truck rental firm in the city. I will call the rental company and get the details on the rented rig. Keep going to the city to get the results from the crime lab and we will talk when you get back," stated Red.

Asadi continued his trip and arrived at the crime lab shortly after hanging up with Red. He went inside the building to pick up the information, and then would head back to Crenna immediately. The lab tech gave him a quick overview:

- The same gun was used to kill Paul Crenna and the EMT hiding in the office. The tech theorizes the gun used was a Glock 43.

- The urine, found in the thicket in direct line to where Paul was standing when he was shot, was that of a female.
- They were able to extract DNA from the blood found on the piece of wood protruding from one of the log piles. This DNA and its match were very telling.
- The majority of the casings found were from the Russian AK-12 rifle fired from the helicopter by the men who attacked Asadi in the woods the night Paul Crenna was murdered.

Asadi took all the documentation, placed it into his car and began the trip back to Crenna. For the return trip he took the main road. This would allow him to get to Crenna quicker than the back road he had taken on the way into the city. As he sped down the highway, Asadi was deep in thought about the information he had just received from the crime lab. As he came out of one of the road's sharper corners, Asadi was confronted with a devastating sight. Alannah's car was on the other side of the road. He saw the mangled rear end and two bodies on the ground, one on either side of the car. Asadi slammed on the brakes, and his car slid to a twisting stop. He exited the car with his gun drawn and saw Alannah. Her head was leaning to the right with the edge of the air bag keeping it from falling forward. First, Asadi opened the driver's side door to make sure Alannah was breathing. He then scanned the car, and the area, for others. It was then that he realized the car seat was empty and Elmear was nowhere in sight. He quickly determined the two men on the ground outside the car were dead. Now that he was sure the scene was secure, Asadi ran to his car to get his cell phone. The first call he made was to get a medical team to the scene as soon as possible. The second call was to Red, and it would be the hardest phone call he had ever had to make in his life.

CHAPTER 18

The Russians transporting the helicopter in the tractor trailer had been lying about their final destination when talking to Asadi. When they were sure that Asadi was far enough ahead of them, they stopped the truck near an open field along the road. The driver put the truck in reverse, backed into the open field, and pulled back onto the road to head in the opposite direction. The rig headed back to the rarely used, overgrown, barely distinguishable dirt road where they had told Asadi that they were turning around. The driver carefully pulled the large rig onto the dirt road, and they slowly began their journey down the mountain path. Their mission was to travel deep into the woods. They were going to leave the truck, and its contents, for Mother Nature to conceal as long as necessary. Someone would return for the truck and its contents when things calmed down in the area. As was proven by the chance meeting with Asadi, it was too dangerous to be on any well-traveled road with this load. If they were pulled over and police checked the load, it could be disastrous for the entire operation. The two men continued to head into the vast forest. Along the way, they passed the vehicle that had been left for them to use to leave the area after their mission was completed.

Very deep into the woods they came across a large pine grove, with a thick layer of pine needles all over the ground. The trees were loaded with low, dead branches extending from their base. The trees were also a good distance apart from each other. The driver turned slightly right and began backing the rig into this grove. Some of the branches broke off, while others bent only to whip back into place as the truck passed by. The branches made scraping sounds as they rubbed the full length of the truck. There were a few scratches, which would not matter. The truck would be well hidden for as long as was needed. The two left the truck unlocked, placing the keys under the driver's side floor mat. Then they started the long walk to their exit vehicle they had passed on the way into the woods. Without cell phone reception, the two would not be able to contact Boris to tell him their task had been complete until they were out of the woods.

Elmear was not with the two men who had hidden the truck containing the helicopter, which earlier had flown her to her place of captivity. Flying below what was considered a safe altitude, the pilot weaved the helicopter through clearings to a cabin located deep in the vast forest. The cabin was owned by the Crenna family. Paul originally suggested they use it to house the various mercenaries they would hire from time to time. Paul was not aware that it would be used as a base for combat operations. If Paul had not been killed by the pile of logs, he would have died by the Russian AK-12s firing from the sky. They decided that they did not need Paul anymore, but they needed Randy at least for a little while longer. Paul had kept the use of the family cabin to himself, so Randy was not aware there were people staying at their vacation home in the woods. This was the very cabin he suggested his mother and sister stay in until he felt things were safer in town. It was at this cabin the helicopter was disassembled, packed and started its journey to safe keeping in the pine grove. It was also the spot where Elmear would be kept.

"This damn kid has not stopped crying since the moment we arrived," screamed one of the captors.

Doctor Svetlana Vladmelov had completed her set of tasks for her husband's mission. She decided it was time to take a much needed vacation from her very public job with the government. In addition to putting up with her insatiable appetite for men, Ivan also had to contend with his dream of fathering an heir being shattered. Along with her routine infidelity came infertility. Svetlana's physical inability to have children did not mean she did not love children, which was exactly why she made her way to the cabin. While she could not give Ivan a male heir, maybe this child would become his heiress. Even before meeting Elmear, Svetlana felt she was the gift of a lifetime, and Svetlana would protect this child with her life. Arriving at the cabin, she exited her car, and heard the baby crying incessantly along with the frustration in her captor's voice.

She threw open the door saying, "Give me the baby you morons. Did you ever think to feed her rather than yell at her?"

Svetlana took Elmear from the man, wrapped her in her arms, and started to sway while talking softly, trying to soothe Elmear. It was not long before Svetlana noticed the real problem.

"OoooWiiiiii! None of you noticed that smell! Get me the diaper bag so I can change this poor little baby," Svetlana snapped.

"What diaper bag?" one of the men asked.

"You mean to tell me you failed to grab the diaper bag so we know what to feed her, and to have clean diapers? Your lack of brains truly amazes me right now! You need to go to the store for diapers and formula. Get three sizes of diapers to fit a six-month old, a one-year old and an eighteen-month old baby. Just get a routine formula, and try not to look confused or ask a clerk for help, which would only make you look conspicuous. Get going, and get your stupid ass back here quickly," Svetlana loudly ordered.

Svetlana continued to soothe Elmear, who eventually calmed at the sound of a soft spoken woman's voice. Svetlana was immediately infatuated with this beautiful little girl. She continued to sway, starring into Elmear's beautiful eyes, and felt connected to this little bundle of love. She had to call Ivan right now.

"Ivan, this baby is beautiful. There has been a change of plans. We are going to keep this wonderful child. This will be the baby I was never able to give you. This will be your heiress. This will be our child. She is so beautiful and took to me right away. This wild plan you devised set us on a new journey. I cannot wait for you to meet our little Anastasia Vladmelov."

At first, Ivan thought his wife had gone off the deep end. He carefully listened to her excitement over this little bundle of joy. Maybe this little girl would tame Svetlana, and create the family he had always wanted. It sounded crazy, but Ivan was all in. He loved the excitement in his wife's voice, and decided right then and there that their new family had been born, and Elmear was now their child!

CHAPTER 19

"Red this is Asadi, please listen carefully. Alannah was involved in both a double shooting, and a car accident. Alannah was not shot, but outside her car there are two dead men with multiple gunshot wounds. Alannah is alive, but appears to have a severe head injury. Her car was hit from behind causing the air bags to activate. Whatever and whoever hit her is no longer around. And Red, Elmear is missing! Her car seat and diaper bag are in the car, but she is not. I have a medical team en route," Asadi relayed to Red as concise and calmly as he could.

Red immediately went into combat mode. While in that mode, he had been trained to control his emotions, think clearly, and move quickly but precisely to achieve the desired results. The results in this case were the safety of his wife and twins growing inside her, the safe return of Elmear, and accountability for everyone involved. These robotic responses made Red appear cold and uncaring, but inside Red was crying out in pain and fear for his family. This is the one mission in life he must accomplish with one hundred percent success; anything less was simply not in the realm of possibility. Asadi recognized this combat reaction, and knew Red was in pain underneath his mission-focused exterior.

"Asadi, please stay at the scene and make sure Alannah is safe. I am leaving now and will make some phone calls on my way to the scene. I am calling in some help. For me to be free to do what may be needed outside the law, I am asking you to take over my position as interim Sheriff! We still need to keep the town safe, but my main focus must be my family right now," explained Red.

"I will do whatever you need Red, but please understand if the situation arises where I have to choose between your family and the town, I will fight with you," replied Asadi.

They ended the call. Red left his badge and service revolver in one of the drawers of his desk at the Sheriff's station. He got in his personal vehicle and removed his personal 9mm from the glove compartment. He took off speeding to the scene of the accident. While driving, Red made a phone call to ask for more help.

"Zach, this is Red. I need help!"

Zach and Layla Morrelli were very close friends of Red and Alannah. They were both heartbroken, and happy, when Red moved his family to Crenna. They were heartbroken over Red's family moving away, but happy for their friends' exciting new adventure. They deserved a fresh start for their growing family as well as for themselves.

The Morrellis were on hiatus trying to determine their lot in life. Financially, they were set, because they had steady income from a medical marijuana store they now owned. They had ventured into their calling as private investigators, but were drawn into cases that were not private investigative in nature. While they did investigate, they always seemed to end up in high profile combative cases, such as the mind altering Chrysalis vaccine, the American war versus China that was fought on American soil, and the international human trafficking ring that had been operating in their town. This was not the private investigative scenario they had imagined. They originally wanted to uncover insurance fraud, out cheating wives or husbands, research financial fraud, etc. They currently felt like government operatives, not private investigators. The Morrellis were trying to decide if they should continue working as private investigators or move on to something new.

Zach and Red had fought in Afghanistan together, forming an unbreakable bond. Their unit in Afghanistan also included the sniper team of Jack Miller and Logan Wilson. Logan was a techie with genius computer skills. This group would go to the ends of the earth to help each other and their families.

Red explained the recent chain of events in Crenna, leading up to the horrific kidnapping of his daughter Elmear, and the attack on his wife Alannah. Zach did not require all the details right then. Red said he needed help and that was enough. Zach would rally the others and they would go to Red's aid immediately.

"We will leave as soon as possible. Let me go so I can alert everyone. I will call you back when we are on the road," replied Zach.

First, Zach informed Layla, who immediately began packing to leave. Zach then called Jack and Logan. Being military, they always had a "ready bag." In addition, they all had packed weapons, while Logan also packed technical gear he thought they might require. Zach and Layla left for Crenna first, with Jack and Logan leaving soon after in a separate vehicle.

Red arrived at the accident scene just as Alannah was being put into the ambulance.

"She is unconscious with a head injury. I don't know how bad it is. Her vitals are good, and they must get her to the hospital quickly. Climb in and go with her so they can leave now. I can handle things here. Once Alannah is stable, call me and I will tell you everything I've discovered here at the scene," suggested Asadi.

Without hesitation Red jumped into the ambulance and they were quickly on the road headed to the hospital. Red could only stare helplessly while the love of his life lay on the gurney fighting for her life. He held her hand and assured her all would be well. Red wondered if Alannah was even aware Elmear was missing. At this point he hoped this was not on her mind, so she could focus on healing herself. Red had lost touch with the God he grew up with. Red felt ashamed because he was now turning to God, asking the all-powerful to heal his wife and guide him to Elmear. His plea was conflicted with violence he could not hide. Red knew that God saw that his path to recovering his baby would be fraught with violence and death. Would God help a man who had left him years ago, and who knew of the violence to come? The silence of these heavy thoughts was broken when Red's phone began to ring.

"Red, we are on the road. Jack and Logan are a few minutes behind us. Where do you want us to go? What can we help with first?" asked Zach.

"Please tell Logan and Jack to meet Asadi at the Sheriff station in town. You and Layla come to the hospital. Asadi is still at the accident scene and has called a few of his State Police friends to help him. Once they arrive, and he briefs them, Asadi will go back to the office to bring Jack and Logan up to speed," replied Red.

"Copy that! We will see you at the hospital. I will call Jack and Logan to alert them where to go," Zach confirmed.

While waiting for the State Police, Asadi received a frantic call from the car repair shop in town. The son, and part owner, had just found his father's lifeless body at the garage. The son was distraught, but able to tell Asadi a few strange things he found. Nothing of immediate value was stolen. The cash register was intact and full. The only thing missing was the Sherriff's squad car that they had just finished repairing. The son thought maybe Asadi had picked the car up from his father while he was out.

Asadi explained to the son that he would be there as soon as possible. There were too many disasters for this "two-man force" to handle right now. As he hung up the phone, a piece of debris caught his eye. It looked like pieces of an emergency flashing light mounted on the front bumper of their squad cars.

The State Police arrived on the scene. Asadi explained what he knew thus far, and asked that they thoroughly finish investigating the area. He asked them to research both of the dead men's identities. Asadi also explained his new thought, that their recently repaired, and now stolen squad car, was involved in this accident. Finding the vehicle involved may lead them to Elmear's location.

Asadi had just received Red's text about him meeting Jack and Logan at the office. He left for town to secure the scene at the car repair station. Once this was under control, he would meet Jack and Logan to enlighten them with details of what had happened over the past few days.

The ambulance arrived at the hospital, Zach and friends are on the way to help, the State Police are investigating the accident scene, God was called upon, and Asadi was handling things in town. For now, all the wheels were in motion, but the real work had yet to begin … they must find the trail that would lead them to Elmear.

CHAPTER 20

Ivan Vladmelov decided to travel to the cabin to see this special little girl who had captured his wife Svetlana's heart. For most people, this trip through the mountain's dirt roads would be a breathtaking journey into the beauty of Mother Nature. For Ivan, it was an arduous voyage filled with dust, filth and backbreaking bumps. In addition to the baby, Ivan had another reason for going to the cabin. He had just been informed that Alannah was still alive, and in the hospital. His instructions to the three men were very clear and concise. Kill the woman, take the baby, and destroy all evidence around the scene. Such incompetence could not be allowed if he were to maintain control over every man and woman in his vast organization.

Ivan's vehicle finally arrived at the cabin, and the driver opened Ivan's door. This aggressive, violent man stepped out the car door into the slightly muddy ground and began making screeching high pitched noises as if he were terrified by something. He quickly jumped back into the car and began yelling at the driver.

"Move the car to a dry area! And where are my spare shoes; mine are now dirty?"

The driver shuffled the car around until he found a dry area, gave Ivan his spare shoes, and once again got out of the car to open Ivan's door.

"Throw these damn shoes away and be more careful next time," Ivan told the driver.

The two men walked to the cabin door, the driver opened the door and Ivan went inside.

"Svetlana, it's me Ivan. Where are you? Where is our new daughter?"

Svetlana did not verbally answer her husband; instead she slowly entered the room smiling, while softly cradling the sleeping baby in her arms.

Ivan walked up to them and a serene feeling came over him. This was a feeling he had not felt in a very long time. To see, and feel his wife's happiness was a strange emotion for him.

"Ivan, sit down in the rocker so you can hold our baby," Svetlana told her husband.

Ivan did as she asked and Svetlana carefully placed Anastasia into his arms.

"Do you like the name I picked out for her? Doesn't Anastasia Vladmelov sound so serene and regal?" Svetlana asked her husband.

"I love the name, my love," replied Ivan.

The minute this little bundle of love hit his arms he just melted. Ivan was truly on an emotional roller coaster with the change in his wife and their new daughter. As he snuggled the baby, his normal internal rage that was constantly brewing seemed to subside. Svetlana sensed a calmer Ivan. She actually witnessed Ivan softening, as he administered justice to the man who did not kill Alannah.

"Hey jackass, get over here," Ivan ordered the man who kidnapped the baby.

"I came here to kill you for not following my orders. I ordered the woman dead, and now I hear she is alive, and in the hospital. Why wasn't she disposed of?" Ivan asked softly.

The man explained Alannah's quick response, and the resulting death of his two partners. He continued by explaining that his only course of action was to crash into her car, grab the baby and get her out of there as quickly as possible.

"You do know I just can't ignore the fact that you did not follow orders. Place your right hand on the table," Ivan told him.

Ivan gave the baby to Svetlana, motioning her to go into the other room with the baby. He then pulled out a knife, walked over to the man, and thrust the knife through his hand, and into the table. There was a quick blood curdling scream and then silence. Ivan pulled out the knife and said, "You wrap that hand up and remember to tell the hospital it was an accident while you were out hunting in the mountains. My driver will take you to the hospital, where you will first find out the condition of the woman and then, if time permits, you can get medical attention for your wound. You remember this the next time you give thought to not following my orders. If there is a next time, it will mean your life!"

The driver and wounded man left. Ivan asked Svetlana to return with the baby, and he sat down to rock their precious child once again. Ivan and Svetlana felt like a real couple. In fact, for the first time, they felt like a family. After this mission, things would change with the Vladmelov's lifestyle. They now had a child to take care of, so things would need to change. This serenity they were both feeling was short. Ivan's phone began ringing. He again handed the baby to Svetlana before answering.

"Boris, how are things going?" Ivan asked.

"The mission is right on schedule, but we are losing men from our security force. The three idiots I sent to watch the Crenna house in case we had to kill one of them were arrested for trespassing, and are now setting in the Crenna jail. These three, plus the man killed from the helicopter, significantly reduces our manpower," replied Boris.

"Well, I can add to that manpower problem, because two of the three men sent to kidnap the child are now dead. We have the baby, but as you said, our security force is all but gone. I will handle this from here Boris. It's time to call in the 'A team' to be sure we all get out of this alive and untouched by the authorities. Hang tight and keep the computer attack going, and I will let you know when to expect help," stated Ivan.

Ivan texted, *"Initiate operation Crenna immediately."*

He hit send and waited. It was not long before he received a reply.

"En route now! Full contingent! Will report as previously arranged; half to cabin and half to Boris."

Ivan called Boris to let him know that help was on the way. He then went back to join his family in the other room. Ivan held his baby Anastasia while he watched his wife just glowing with happiness. This was the life he had always dreamed of with this woman. He must be sure it continued from this point forward.

CHAPTER 21

Tension had been steadily rising in America. It was all happening just as they had planned, because when you tampered with American's money, you struck a nerve that could easily be turned into a violent rage to fight for what they felt belonged to them.

Millions of people, those who depended on receiving a monthly Social Security check, were cut off. The majority of those recipients had been set up for direct deposit, which meant under normal circumstances, they would not immediately be aware that they did not receive their money. Boris' team wanted to be sure these people were aware that they had not received their money, so immediate chaos would ensue. The programmers had the system send a pay stub to all Social Security recipients with the following cryptic message:

"The American government would like to thank each of you for contributing your Social Security funds to the overwhelming influx of helpless immigrants. These much needed funds will be used towards the housing, and the feeding of these downtrodden people from other countries. Again, you have the sincere thanks of your entire government."

The government buildings that handled Social Security funds were suddenly overwhelmed with phone calls, and people were coming in to ask what was going on. All their questions went unanswered, which just added fuel to the anger and mayhem.

State unemployment checks and direct deposits began failing, because the funds were not in the bank. Federal funds, usually directed to each state, were redirected to offshore accounts that had been set up to help fund the Russian government. The unemployed were both panicked and furious that their funds had been cut off without any prior warning.

America's entire military went unpaid. This was handled much the same way as Social Security payments had been handled, except there was a very different message on their pay stub.

"To our military men and women: PLEASE continue to fight for all Americans. This fight has moved from the battlefield to the financial field. Until our government officials can agree on a budget, your pay will go towards keeping vital military operations afloat. This will continue until the budget is approved. Furthermore, you will not receive any back pay."

All Medicare, Medicaid, and other healthcare funding were depleted. The money from the various government accounts was now missing. The Russian military had just received the largest financial infusion in its entire history from the transfer of all these funds. The medical profession was in a state of turmoil. The flow of money from those government accounts that were needed to keep the hospitals and other medical offices afloat had been completely blocked.

Even the little backwoods town of Crenna was oozing with tension, anger and the banter of revolt could be heard. The plan Paul had designed was working, and if not stopped soon, the nation would be in total chaos!

"Abigail, will you please reconsider and leave with me to go to our cabin. I don't know what has happened to our family, but I believe Randy is trying to help us, so let's accept his help and leave now," Lily implored.

"Mom, we have not been a family for a very long time. You would not like what I have become, and as I already told you, I am not leaving this town before I get what's mine. You go to the cabin. I am fully capable of taking care of myself," replied Abigail stubbornly.

"I should have left Paul, and this town, years ago! It's blatantly obvious that you could not care less about what happens to me. I guess this will take me out of the running for the 'mother of the year' award, but I am leaving town. I am <u>not</u> going to the cabin, and I really don't know where I am going right now. You have my cell phone number if you, or Randy, ever want to contact me in the future. I want nothing from this place anymore, so if money is worth more than life to you, then by all means enjoy your battle," Lily said to her daughter as she walked out of the house for the last time.

Ivan called Boris with news of reinforcements. "Boris, our six best fighting men are on the way. Three will come to me at the cabin, and three will come to you in town. Mikhail, whom you already know, is leading these men. He is a brutal man who we want to make sure is on our side. I will send you his contact information. What do you think our exposure is with our three imbeciles in the town jail?"

"They need to either be released from jail on bail or released from life. I do not trust them to keep their mouths shut. Right now the cops are too busy to worry about them, but eventually they will be questioned, and I am worried about what they might say," replied Boris.

"When the new men arrive, you do what you think is best. I will leave this decision up to you. We will talk later," Ivan said as he clicked off the call.

Boris would have to determine how to kill these three, because he knew they would not be released from jail before they were questioned.

CHAPTER 22

Alannah underwent a barrage of medical testing at the hospital. The doctor indicated that it appeared that she had been hit by a corner of the air bag, and the steering wheel. The precarious position, which had been created when Alannah leaned down to get her cell phone, had caused part of her head to strike the steering wheel. The doctor went on to explain the tests showed slight traumatic brain injury, but he felt that she would fully recover. The doctor admitted he was confused that Alannah was still unconscious, and worried it may be psychological. Red explained the fact that their baby girl was missing, which furthered the doctor's feeling it was her mind keeping Alannah unconscious. The doctor indicated Alannah may be shutting down her consciousness to avoid dealing with the sheer anguish that her daughter had been kidnapped. All they could do now was watch her vitals, and give her time to come out of this medical trauma.

Zach and Layla pulled into the hospital parking lot, got out of the car and headed to the emergency room. Inside they were told that Alannah had been admitted, and after testing had been placed in room 3211. The hospital volunteer pointed to the elevators, and gave them directions to follow when they arrived on the third floor. As the couple was coming down the hall, Red saw them and let out a huge sigh of relief.

"It's so good to see you two! I can't tell you how much it means to us having you here," Red told the Morrellis.

"It's good to see you Red, but I wish it were under different circumstances. How is Alannah?" asked Layla.

Red went over all the information he had been given by the doctor.

"Can we go in and see her? How are you holding up Red?" Layla asked

"Absolutely, let's go to her room. She is not responding, but the doctor says it's important to talk to her. As for me, I am not handling this very well at all. My daughter is missing and my wife won't wake up from her head injury. I need to find my daughter, but don't want to leave my wife's side," Red explained.

"One thing at a time Red. Let's go in and see Alannah first," suggested Layla.

The sight of Alannah lying in bed lifeless, hooked up to machines and IVs took Zach and Layla's breathe away. Layla knew that Alannah was a strong woman, and would fight to remain with her family.

After investigating the scene at the garage, Asadi was convinced that the owner had been murdered once the killers found what they had come for: the newly repaired Sheriff's squad car. The assailants knew that once Alannah recognized the patrol car, she would have pulled over without hesitation. No evidence at the garage would lead them to the killers, so for now this information was just another piece of the puzzle. Asadi left the garage to go meet Jack and Logan at the Sheriff's office.

It was good timing, because just as Asadi pulled up to the station, Jack and Logan pulled in behind him.

"Jack. Logan. Wow, it is so great to see you guys again," Asadi yelled as he got out of his car and saw his two friends.

Afghanistan was both a time they wanted to forget, and a time they forged friendships that would last a lifetime. These men had all served together on the battlefield, and now they would work together to uncover what was going on in this beautiful, small town.

"Come on inside. You guys will work out of here, and the two of you will stay at my place. Logan, I assume you brought your gadgets, so you can set up in the room we use for eating, interrogating, and napping," Asadi chuckled as he showed them around.

Before Asadi could begin updating Jack and Logan, his phone rang. It was Red, and Asadi hoped he had some better news.

"Hi Red. How is Alannah?"

Red explained what he knew about Alannah's condition, and then asked Asadi to give him a situational update. Asadi brought him up to speed, highlighting the car garage owner's murder, and squad car theft, both of which Red had known nothing about.

"I would suggest Logan set up his gear in our all-purpose room, then see if he can get a lock on the stolen squad car. Our squad car radios are wired so they are constantly on. As long as the power button on the radio unit is in the 'on' position we have a means of tracking the location of the car. It's a long shot, but I think it's worth a try. Jack and I will go back to the accident scene, check in with the

State Police, and then look around the area for the stolen squad car. If we can locate our car we might get a lead on where these people were going," Asadi suggested to Red.

"Sounds good Asadi. Just make sure Logan is armed and stays vigilant. We still have three prisoners who are somehow involved. As soon as I can break away, I want to interrogate the three of them," replied Red.

Logan began setting up his gear as discussed, while Jack and Asadi left to go to the accident scene.

Red never left Alannah's side, continuing to hold her hand so that she knew he was there with her.

Layla heard Red's reply to Asadi and felt she had to speak up.

"Red, I completely understand why you want to stay, but I am asking you to leave. I want you to trust me to take care of, and protect Alannah. Let me do this so you and Zach can find your daughter. You two go do what you do best, dig deep, and do whatever you must to bring Elmear home."

With the simple gentle squeeze of her hand, Alannah made it clear that he was ok to leave. One soft squeeze said I love you, and go find our daughter.

Red wiped away a tear, looked at Zach and Layla saying, "Thank you Layla. Take my pistol just in case. I will grab my other pistol in the car. Let's go get my daughter, Zach." He bent over and kissed Alannah, told her he loved her and left for the most important mission of his lifetime.

Red and Zach walked to the bank of elevators, pushed the down button and waited for one to arrive. They heard a *"ding,"* the elevator doors opened and people exited the elevator. The last man off the elevator was holding his hand wrapped in a blood-soaked towel. Blood dripped onto the floor as the man had begun to walk down the hall. Red would not ignore a person in need, and had stopped to provide him directions to the right department for medical attention.

"Sir, the emergency room is downstairs, hop back in and we will take you there. We are going right by there anyway," Red suggested to the wounded man.

"Thank you officer, but I have to be sure my wife is alright before I can worry about myself. They have just brought her up here. I will be alright, it looks worse than it really is, but thank you for the offer," the man replied in very broken English.

The wounded man quickly turned and started down the hallway. Red gave Zach a confused look, and then let the elevator doors shut. Soon the two men were in the car headed for the Sheriff station to begin their quest for Elmear.

CHAPTER 23

Boris had the Sheriff's station under intense surveillance ever since he found out his three men were in jail. Due to his shortage of security people, Boris could not have the building watched 24/7. Even with this limited monitoring, Boris felt he had enough information to pass to Mikhail, information which would allow his men to complete the task of silencing the three Russian prisoners.

"There are only two officers in the entire Sheriff's department. One is in the hospital with his wife, who really should be dead. The second was hunkered down watching over our three men in the jail. With all the activity around town the deputy has had to leave the three prisoners alone while he takes care of official business. When we see him leave again this will give you the opportunity to go in and take care of those idiots," Boris explained to Mikhail.

"When the time comes, what have you decided? Do you want me to bring the three to you, do you want them left dead in their cell to send a message, or do you want them to disappear?" asked Mikhail.

"Make them disappear forever. In addition, you must find their belongings. Typically the American police put all prisoners' belongings into a manila envelope. We need to find all three of these envelopes to be sure their phones and identification disappear along with their bodies," rasped Boris.

Lily turned right onto the dirt road and began the rugged trip up to their family cabin. Going to the cabin, after she had told Abigail she was not going, was a last minute decision. This spur of the moment decision was driven by whatever mother's love and instinct was left inside Lily. She realized she could not just totally leave the area with her children still involved in conflict, even though she had no idea what they were involved in, or how bad it might be.

Lily turned left onto another dirt road and unbeknownst to her, someone was watching her make the turn. The mystery man immediately alerted others up the road that an intruder was headed towards the cabin. After traveling another slow mile, Lily turned slight right onto yet another dirt road riddled with rocks, bumps and ruts. Just as her vehicle came out of the turn she was faced with two men in the middle of the road, both with pistols pointed at her. One of the men got into the passenger seat and told Lily to continue driving to the cabin.

Once in the car, the man spoke into his walkie-talkie, "We have her sir. We will be at your location in a few minutes."

Lily was scared to death, and sorry she had made the split-second decision to go to the cabin. She wondered who these men were, and why they were on their property. Her questions would be answered soon, because they were approaching the Crenna family cabin. Lily stopped the car, and was ordered to get out and go into the cabin.

The moment she opened the cabin door, the answer to "who" was obvious, but she had no earthly idea why Ivan would take her prisoner.

"Well, hello Mrs. Crenna. To what do I owe the pleasure of your visit?" Ivan asked Lily.

"No, the real question is why are you trespassing on our property? Why are these people guarding this place as if it were a fortress?" asked Lily.

"It's obvious you, and your deceased husband, were not communicating, like most loving couples do. You know, like Svetlana and I communicate! Your husband suggested that we use this secluded area as our secure base of operations," replied Ivan.

"Why would you need a secure location? You are part of a logging company, not some international crime group. You act like some mafia crime boss. You invested in our company, and I am sure before Paul died, he regretted allowing you to invest," Lily hotly replied as she became more and more terrified.

"Since you will never leave this place alive, you should know there are things going on in this town that will impact the very structure of your American society. I could care less about your little logging company or this backwoods town. Your husband and son are the men who created the means to ratchet up the violence in America. Our election interference was just the start, and you Americans learned nothing from that attack. This interference is so much bigger and better, thanks to your dear, dead husband, Paul," explained Ivan.

"So, it was your men who killed Paul, and shot everything in sight from the helicopter," Lily questioned.

"Actually, no it was not us! My men reported Paul was down when our grand entrance took place. He was the target because he was becoming spineless. He wanted to back out of our deal and stop the process, which I would not allow. I really have no idea who killed him, but if I did know I would thank them for sure," Ivan evilly cackled.

Ivan was interrupted by the sound of a ringing phone. At first no one knew where the ringing phone was located, and then Ivan realized it was somewhere in Lily's possession.

"Lily my dear, please hand me your phone." Ivan asked.

Lily reached into her back pocket and handed the phone to Ivan who looked at the caller ID and hit the answer icon.

"Well hello Randy. How are things going at the shop?" Ivan asks sarcastically.

There was a long pause while Randy gathered his thoughts on how to respond to Ivan.

"Things are going well, as I am sure Boris has informed you already. I was calling to talk with my mother, and imagine my surprise when you answered her phone," replied Randy breathlessly.

"Well Randy, you were warned if you did not co-operate with us, we would be forced to kill a family member. It's difficult to admit, but my incompetent security people watching your mother's home were arrested by the police. Then to my surprise your mother decided to come to the family cabin, which your father failed to mention we were occupying. I am also guessing your father failed to mention this fact to you as well, correct?" Ivan asked.

"True, but I still do not understand why you continue to make these threats. I have not skipped a beat. Everything happened just as we designed, and just as you asked," Randy says.

"Insurance my boy. Insurance! You continue to hold up your end of the bargain and your mother will be just fine. Now it is time for you to get back to work," replied Ivan as he disconnected the call, then slammed down the phone.

"Make yourself at home Mrs. Crenna. You are going to be our guest for a long while," sneered Ivan.

Randy hung up the phone and headed back to the only secure area in the building. Once in the bathroom, he quickly pulled out his phone and texted, *"Abort pickup. Repeat, abort pickup. Will be in touch soon."* He hit send and quickly went back to work.

CHAPTER 24

One of the floor nurses came into Alannah's room with her meds and a syringe to administer a sedative. Seeing this syringe, Layla became a little concerned, so she began asking questions.

"Could you tell me what medicine you plan to inject into Alannah?"

"The doctor suspects Alannah is still unconscious because she does not want to face the reality of her daughter's disappearance. This syringe contains a sedative for her, which is counter intuitive to normal thinking of ways to help her awaken. Even though she is unconscious, her missing daughter has put Alannah into a state of high stress. If we can calm her thoughts, and body, we believe she will come to terms with the tragedy, and regain consciousness ready to fight. Even if this does not work as we hoped, the sedative will not harm her in anyway," the nurse explained.

Before Layla could thank the nurse for the detailed information, the hospital's loudspeaker system started bellowing, "Code blue third floor. All code blue team members report to room 3001 stat!"

The nurse, obviously a member of this team, left the syringe and meds on the tray right next to Alannah, and then ran towards room 3001 as instructed. On one hand, Layla felt the nurse was very knowledgeable and pleasant. On the other hand, she questioned the nurse's professionalism for just leaving meds out in the open before leaving the room. There was a flurry of activity out in the hallway, as team members hurried to the code blue location. Layla was not a medical professional, but she was skeptical about the timing of the code blue emergency. Her skepticism resulted from a text Zach sent to her as he, and Red were leaving the hospital. The text contained a photo, along with Zach's description of what happened. The text, plus the fact that this emergency happened shortly after Zach sent the photo of the wounded man walking down the hall, had given Layla an uneasy feeling. Added to these issues was the fact that anyone could push the code blue button in any of the hospital's many rooms, and that thought put Layla on even higher alert! Her neck was tingling, indicating she had a very bad, gut feeling of doom.

Alannah's hospital room had two curtains running down the middle that stretched around the end of each bed. If two people occupied the space the curtains would close to provide privacy for both patients. Alannah was in the bed closest to the window in the room. The bed closest to the hospital room's door was now empty. Since it was only Alannah in the room, both curtains were partially open. Layla moved her chair into a position that kept her hidden from anyone entering the room. If necessary, this would give her the ability to react without being seen.

Layla's skepticism was founded when she heard someone enter Alannah's room. There he was, the man with the blood soaked hand in the photo that Zach had sent to Layla earlier. Unbeknownst to Layla, this was one of the men who Ivan originally had sent to kill Alannah. He was now trying to carry out his second chance to kill Alannah, which was also his only chance to live. This bloodied, weak man was now standing in front of Alannah's lifeless body. This was the very reason Zach had alerted Layla with a text. He grabbed a pillow from the empty bed, and slowly bent over Alannah with the blood soaked pillow in his hands. He was lowering it over her face when Layla slowly moved from the shadows and placed the barrel of her gun on the side of his head.

"Make no sudden moves, stand up slowly and throw the pillow to the floor," Layla instructed him. At first he did not comply, because at this point he knew he would either die at Ivan's hand or by the gun now pointed at his head.

"Give me a reason to kill you!" hissed Layla.

All of a sudden, Alannah's eyes opened and the first thing she saw was the wretched man who had tried to kill her, and who had taken her baby. With the speed and accuracy of a trained warrior, she grabbed the syringe the nurse had left, and forced the needle into his thigh releasing the medication. The man winced in pain, grabbed his thigh and fell to the floor sedated and useless.

"Well, good morning buttercup! It's good to see you awake," Layla quipped.

"Layla, this is the man who rammed into my car and took Elmear. The only reason I didn't kill him on the spot was that he could lead us to Elmear. Please get the nurse and see if there is something they can give him to wake him up quickly," Alannah asked Layla.

The nurse came into the room mumbling, "Some jackass pushed the code blue button for no reason. There was no emerg ..."

Before she could finish her sentence, the nurse saw the man on the floor, and Layla standing there with a gun in her hand.

"It's ok nurse. This man was going to kill me, and Layla stopped him. It's a long story, and I know it's hard to believe, but if you would call my husband, he will clear all this up. If you would be more comfortable, call hospital security, because they know my family, and my husband Red, who is the Sheriff of Crenna. This man abducted my child, and we need him awake as soon as possible, because he could lead us to where my daughter has been taken. I injected the sedative in the syringe you were going to give me. Is there anything you can give him to wake him now as opposed to waiting for the sedative to wear off?" Alannah asked the nurse.

Layla had already pulled her phone out to alert Zach of the situation. He and Red were at the scene of the accident talking with the State Police. They immediately jumped into the car and headed back to the hospital. This could be the big break they needed to find

Elmear. Red had to get this man to talk, and Zach knew he had to be sure that Red did not kill the man while trying to get this information.

Ivan's driver was in the hospital parking lot waiting for their man to return with news that Alannah was dead. Instead, he saw Red flying back into the parking lot and quickly run into the same hospital he had left only a short time ago. This was not good news, and the driver alerted Ivan of this development.

"He's been in there for quite awhile. I think something's gone wrong because the Sheriff just returned and went inside," the driver told Ivan.

"Get out of there now and I will send one of Mikhail's sharp shooters to get the job done once and for all," replied Ivan.

CHAPTER 25

Paul Crenna had bucked the American system his entire life, unlike the other Crenna men before him. His father and all the Crenna patriarchs before his father were staunch American patriots. They were patriots who had refused to be defined in association with a particular political party. They believed people should enter politics to serve the people not a specific political party and its agenda. Whatever political candidate's agenda would be best for the people of Crenna became the family's choice. Political party was of no concern. It was often said in the nation's political world that, "as Crenna votes, so goes the rest of the country." Every Crenna patriarch before Paul had fought in one of America's wars, and they did it with pride. Paul chose not to join his family's military elite simply because, "It was just not for him."

Paul blamed his vitriol of the government on everything from Omicron to lazy people to woke politics. The real blame was with himself; an irrational, self serving, arrogant, incompetent, defiant man, Paul Crenna. Something in Paul had made him revolt against everything his predecessors had worked and fought to uphold. Paul's lack of patriotism was simply his way of showing contempt, and dishonor towards prior generations of his family. Behind his back, everyone had tried making excuses for Paul's rebellious behavior. "Oh, it is because his mother did not breast feed him; he was acting out, crying for his father's attention; he was a drug addict in college and it affected his brain," and on and on. The unfortunate reality was that society simply had "bad eggs" everywhere! It was true, Paul was a drug addict for a period of time, but that was not the reason for his hatred of his family and his country. During this drug-induced time, rather than support his efforts to get clean, his family berated his behavior for embarrassing his father, and their proud family history. This just solidified Paul's need to retaliate, and to destroy America in the worst way he could find.

Well into his plan to enter the government's computer system, Paul realized the project was way too big for just one person to handle. Enter Ivan! As smart as Paul was, he lacked common sense when he partnered with Ivan. Ivan participated using the guise of investing in the logging company. He connived his way into Paul's life, and his project. Coincidentally, Ivan had the same goals of bringing chaos to America. Here was where the lower achieving people, with excessive common sense, would have questioned Ivan's existence in the small, remote town of Crenna.

Paul brought his son, Randy, into the programming group, both because of his programming skill and Paul's desire to have his son share in his plan to destroy America. To Randy, Ivan's involvement in this plan was too coincidental and staged. A Russian billionaire traveling with a full contingent of highly trained Russian thugs and a team of Russian hackers picked Crenna to visit?

"Really?" thought Randy. Randy's common sense led him to be mistrustful of his father, and Ivan. Randy often speculated if Ivan was working for his own interests, Russia's interest, or in the interest of a mysterious group lurking in the shadows? It no longer mattered, because Randy was not on board with this program to cripple America, and sought outside help some time ago. He first tried to convince his father that his plan should be abandoned, but to no avail.

Right now Randy was trapped. His life, his mother's life, and his sister's life depended on him continuing to please Ivan and Ivan's superiors, whoever they were! The help that Randy had reached out for was now silent. He had asked to have himself and his family pulled from this mess, but he had received no confirmation. He aborted this request when he found out his mother was being held by Ivan. There was also no response to this message. Randy knew he had to devise his own plan to get him and his family out of this crazy situation alive.

Boris received word that Asadi had left headquarters with a second unknown person. This meant the three prisoners had been left alone. Boris alerted Mikhail that their plan was a go.

Since the government money had dried up, the people in Crenna were frustrated, upset and were taking to the streets. There was only one government office in town, which took the brunt of the townspeople's displeasure. This was a small building housing the Office of Forestry, which was a part of the United States government Agricultural department. This division had nothing to do with the government payments to its citizens, but because it was a part of the government, it was now under assault. People were frantically calling the office, and trying to get inside to find out where their money was. The workers inside were frightened by everyone's anger, and had placed a call to the Sheriff's department for help. With Red at the hospital and Asadi and Jack searching for the squad car, Logan and the three prisoners were the only people left at the Sheriff's headquarters. Logan did not answer the phones right away, but when they continued to incessantly ring he decided it best to answer them. Hearing what was happening; Logan then contacted Asadi who had no choice but to return to town.

Mikhail sent two of his men to the Sheriffs headquarters to grab the three prisoners and their belongings, as Boris had instructed. They were unaware that Logan was inside, because when Jack and Logan arrived, no one had been watching the area. Boris did not have the manpower to watch the headquarters twenty four hours a day. Mikhail's two assailants went to the back door of the Sheriff's station, and walked right through the unlocked door. The doors were never locked in this small town, and the building did not have an alarm system. Logan's wartime training heightened his senses, and he was always on alert for trouble. He heard the back door click shut and knew it was too soon for Asadi to have returned to town. Logan grabbed his pistol, clicked off the safety and moved out of view behind the opened office door.

Boris's imprisoned men were overjoyed at the sight of their rescuers. Mikhail's men asked if they noticed where their jailers had placed the keys to their cell. One of the prisoners pointed to the room where Logan had been setting up his equipment. The prisoners were pointing to quietly tell their comrades that Asadi had put the keys somewhere in that room. Mikhail's men felt that this silent method of communication may be indicating that someone else was in the building. Logan eyed the keys hanging on the wall right next to him. One of the men entered the room; Logan slowly raised his gun aiming it at the intruder. The man slowly scanned the room and eventually came face to face with Logan. Without hesitation the man ducked, jumping to his left with his gun out, and fired at Logan. In the same instant Logan mirrored the move, jumping to his left, and fired back. Logan's bullets hit the mark and the man fell lifelessly to the floor. The second man started shooting, but not at Logan. He began executing the three caged prisoners, who had nowhere to go, and nowhere to hide. Logan dove out of the office, and began shooting at the second man. This second assailant chose to run and not return fire. He left through the front door and was met outside by Asadi and Jack who quickly pinned him down without firing a shot. Logan ran out to see the man cuffed with Asadi pulling him back to an upright position.

"Asadi we need medical staff here as soon as possible. This guy came in and just started shooting the men in the cell. There was a second man, but he is inside, dead. What the hell is going on here in your little town? All these guys sound and look Russian," Logan said to Asadi.

"I wish I knew Logan! I plan to get some answers, but I think it will all lead back to Ivan Vladmelov," replied Asadi.

CHAPTER 26

Ivan's sharpshooter was set up on the roof across from the hospital. Ivan decided it was no longer necessary to kill Alannah, because he now had Elmear to use as his bargaining chip. The new target was now the man who had failed Ivan twice. He had had two chances to kill Alannah and botched both attempts.

Red and Zach arrived at the hospital, and sprinted through the emergency room doors into the hospital. Zach was pushing himself to keep up with Red whose adrenaline had kicked in ten fold. Red was angry, scared and out for blood. The intruder represented the men who had taken his baby, endangered his wife and their unborn twins. Zach knew he had to find the strength to catch up with Red, making sure that Red did not kill the very person who may know where Elmear had been hidden. Rather than wait for an elevator, Red threw open the door to the stairway and started running up to the third floor. Just as Zach was about to pass the bank of elevators, one of them opened! Zach jumped inside, pushed the close doors button repeatedly and hit the third floor button.

The elevators were located closer to Alannah's room than were the stairs that Red had taken. When the elevator reached the third floor, the doors opened and Zach rushed through them, turning toward Alannah's room. He saw Red barreling towards him in the hallway. Zach had reached Alannah's door just before Red, and placed his body in the center of her room's doorway as a human blockade.

"Red, please stop for just one moment! You can't kill this guy; he is the one man who has information about your daughter. You check on Alannah, and let me handle this guy for now. Can you please do this?"

Red glared angrily at Zach, and for a moment seemed to look right through him as if he had not been listening to anything. Suddenly, Red came to his senses, and realized Zach was right. Red thanked God Zach was there to stop him, because he would have attacked the enemy, "I'm good Zach! You are right; let's get inside."

Red went inside the room and the vision of Alannah alert and sitting up, brought tears to his eyes.

"Are you ok? Are the babies ok? Can we go home?" Red rambled emotionally.

"Red, please slow down. We are all fine. Physically I am good, and the babies have not been affected," Alannah began to cry as she continued, "But Red, I lost our baby Elmear. I killed two of those bastards, but lost sight of the third man as I was searching for my phone during the altercation. That awful man in the chair next to the security guards took our sweet baby," Alannah said, pointing to Ivan's man who had tried to kill her.

"Alannah, none of this was your fault. You did not lose Elmear; she was taken from you. I swear we will get her back. Layla will stay with you while Zach and I get some answers from this scumbag. Please let me do this. You take care of yourself and our babies. Just remember, without you I am nothing. So please try to stay focused on yourself and the twins, and I will keep Layla posted," pleaded Red as he leaned down and kissed Alannah, holding her to his chest.

"Is there a private room where we can question this moron immediately?" Zach asked the hospital security people.

Zach, Red and the assailant left Alannah's room and followed the security team to their office area in the hospital. Zach and Red went into the room with their prisoner while hospital security stood guard outside the door.

"We can do this the easy way, or we can do it the hard way. It's up to you," growled Red.

Zach decided he should take over, because Red had begun to boil over with emotion.

"Let's start by you telling us who you are," Zach began.

"My name is of no consequence to you," he replied defiantly in accented broken English.

"That's really true. I don't care who you are, but what I do care about is where my daughter has been taken and who you are working for," Red replied now standing face to face with this man he did not know, as he trembled under the effort of holding back.

"I am in an impossible situation. When my superiors find out I have failed to murder your wife for the second time, they will kill me. If I give you the information you need, my superiors will kill me. If I don't give you the information you want, I will eventually end up in the prison system, where my superiors have access to many imprisoned killers, who would kill me for the chance to get out of jail, and work for these people. So you see, it would appear I am dead no matter what path I chose," he replied logically with his head down.

"So it seems impossible to reach any thread of morality that might be left inside you to ask that you help me get my daughter back. If I knew of a way to guarantee it, I would protect you, but without knowing who we are dealing with, I cannot make that guarantee," replied Red.

"The things I have done for these people have wiped out my conscience and anything that may have been good inside of me. You have no idea how powerful these people are. These people do not work for governments, they control governments. What governments is the question and the obvious answer is not always the correct answer," explained the prisoner in a very evasive manner.

Red's phone began ringing, "Asadi is everything ok?" Red asked.

Asadi explained what had taken place at headquarters. They now had three dead prisoners, one dead assailant and one new prisoner.

"Thank God the three of you are ok! We have had an issue at the hospital as well. Alannah is awake, and doing well physically. The man who rammed into Alannah's car and kidnapped Elmear attempted to kill Alannah in the hospital. We have the assailant in custody, but he has not revealed any information. I'm going to have hospital security transport him to headquarters, and we will question him again later," Red told Asadi.

"Send him over. One of us will stay with the two prisoners, while the others go back out to search for the squad car and Elmear. Logan will probably stay here, because he has been setting up his gear," replied Asadi.

Red asked the two security guards to take the prisoner to the Sheriff's station. He explained that Asadi would be there to take custody, so they could immediately return to their hospital duties. Each guard grabbed one of the prisoner's arms, and walked him down the hall leading to the parking lot. As they exited the hospital, gunfire erupted, and it was over in less than five seconds. The two guards did not hear a thing, but felt the prisoner go limp, falling to the sidewalk with two bullet holes in his chest. The holes were directly in line with the heart, so his death was immediate. They never saw nor heard the sniper.

The security guards yelled, "Take cover!" One guard took cover to remain on the scene, while the other ran back into the hospital to alert Red. Knowing the job was completed, the sharpshooter picked up the two shell casings, put his weapon in its case, and moved from his shooting position to coolly leave the area.

CHAPTER 27

Red was full of unimaginable anxiety, and felt totally defeated when he heard that their best source of information to recover Elmear had just been professionally executed.

"We have to move Alannah's bed away from the window," Red yelled out loud.

Everyone scrambled to rearrange the room to ensure her safety.

"This is Red Kelly, from Crenna. Can you send assistance to guard a room at the hospital as soon as possible?" Red asked the State Police over the phone.

Red then alerted Asadi of the distressing situation.

"Layla and Alannah, are you still ok if we leave now to find Elmear? The State Police are sending people to help guard the area so you will not be alone," promised Red.

"Red, get going. We will be fine. I know Layla has a weapon, but please leave me one as well. You must find our daughter!" Alannah replied.

Red left Alannah his pistol. He would grab another weapon that he stored in his car. Red and Zach left the hospital once again to begin desperately searching for Elmear.

The one and only prisoner remaining was placed in the Crenna jail cell. Before they headed back out to look for the missing squad car, and Elmear, Asadi and Jack backtracked to the forestry office. Asadi wanted to get a firsthand look at what had been happening. There were people milling around everywhere outside the building. A few were at the front door banging on the window trying to get someone's attention.

"Why are you banging on the window when the sign clearly indicates the office is closed?" Asadi asked the people at the door.

"All of us outside went unpaid by our wonderful government. We have no money, no job and no one is explaining to us why this has happened. This is the only government office in town, and they should have contacts to get us some answers," one of the people in the crowd replied.

"Banging down the doors is not going to get you answers from an office that has nothing to do with government payments. You all need to clear out, go home and contact the appropriate office by phone. All you are accomplishing here is that you are frightening the people inside who are probably your neighbors and friends," Asadi announced.

Asadi did not know how long the angry crowd would stay away. There was a feeling of tension in the air all throughout the town. With Red out of the mix, Asadi might have to stay in town if things continued to worsen. He and Jack were walking back to their car when they saw a figure walking from the dispersing crowd. The hooded figure walked directly towards Asadi in a very committed, but suspicious manner. Head down, both hands were inside the hoody pockets and the person appeared to be keenly focused on walking to Jack and/or Asadi.

"Are you seeing this?" Jack said to Asadi.

"Yes," replied Asadi.

The two men kept their stride, but began to separate to see if the figure would change direction, plus this separation would create a better tactile advantage for them. Sure enough the person's path drifted toward Asadi. Jack stopped to provide stability if shooting became necessary. The mystery figure stopped at a trash can before reaching Asadi. The person nodded their head in an up and down "yes" motion, pulled what looked like a folder from under the hoody, and slid it through the opening of the trash can. The strange figure then turned right, and disappeared back into the crowd.

Knowing they could not immediately go to the trash can to retrieve the folder, Asadi and Jack headed to their vehicle to discuss what to do next.

"Do you have any idea who that might have been?" Jack asked Asadi.

"I have no idea. By the way they moved, I felt like it was a man, but it's only a guess right now," replied Asadi.

"How do you want to play this," asked Jack.

"Between this strange incident, and the unruly crowds, I think I need to stay here. I will give it some time, then go pull the object out of the trash. Do you know the accident scene area well enough to keep searching for the squad car involved in hitting Alannah?" Asadi asked Jack.

"Yes, I am sure I can find my way around. I am more worried about leaving you here because you know that crowd will eventually return," Jack stated.

"I know these people, so I hope that's in my favor. We really need to split up to keep one of us looking for any clues telling us where Elmear may have been taken. Go ahead and take my car, I am close enough to walk to headquarters if necessary," Asadi answered.

Jack finally agreed, got into the squad car and headed back to the scene of Alannah's accident. He remembered seeing a few dirt roads in the area, and thought they would be a good place to start his search. Jack began meandering through the beautiful countryside, wishing he were doing this under different circumstances. As he drove down the entrance to one of the dirt roads, Jack stopped to look around before venturing any further. Immediately something caught his eye in the dirt. He saw the tracks of a car that had obviously slid onto the dirt road from the main road. The tracks showed a sliding curved path indicating the brakes had been overused as the car cornered into the dirt road. Jack then noticed that as the tracks straightened, the front left tire track became irregular. He suspected this irregularity indicated that the tire was almost flat, if not completely flat. He quickly returned to the car and grabbed his phone.

"Red, can you meet me near Alannah's accident scene?" Jack asked.

"Absolutely! We were just leaving the hospital. Our one, good lead is now dead, which I will explain later. Where are you, and did you find something?" Red asked Jack.

"We may have a better lead. I'm about two miles south of the actual scene. There's a dirt road on the right hand side. I believe our missing vehicle may have gone down this road," replied Jack.

"Zach and I will meet you there," Red told Jack as they got into their car and headed off to meet Jack.

CHAPTER 28

"I hire all these highly trained, so-called mercenaries and warriors, and they are getting their asses kicked all over town. Six of them are now dead, one is in jail, and they are being defeated by two country bumpkin cops and their band of merry men. You need to live up to your reputation Mikhail! See there no more of our men are killed, and that we have no additional security breaches," Ivan demanded over the phone.

"You need to be careful with whom you are mouthing off to, Ivan my friend. I don't answer to you, and you did not hire me! I was assigned to be sure you complete your mission for our country. Once you are done all bets are off. So change your approach, or watch your back when this is all over, big man," replied Mikhail.

Ivan quickly ended the call without saying another word. Naturally he was furious, because he was not used to being spoken to in that manner. Ivan was in fact enraged, and also somewhat afraid, but he would never admit to anyone that he felt that way.

"Svetlana, we need to be ready to get out of here in a moment's notice! Things are nearing an end in this godforsaken town. Make sure you, and our baby, are ready to go when I give the word," Ivan explained.

"We are both ready to go now, my love! Anastasia's necessities are neatly packed in her diaper bag. Anything I own in this demon country can be left behind; everything is soiled with the memories of places I despise. And I know my baby will let me 'shop until I drop' when this is all over!" replied Svetlana.

Ivan smiled, still basking in the glow of their newfound loving relationship. If this continued, Ivan would try to give this woman anything she wanted. But make no mistake, at this point he knew Svetlana still could not be trusted not to seduce the next scent of pheromones who came wafting her way.

Asadi continued to watch the area around the trash can containing the folder that was dumped by the mysterious person. The crowd around the forestry office did not totally disperse as Asadi had requested. They began moving away hoping Asadi would leave, but once they saw he was staying, they began wandering back into the area.

Asadi was now experiencing déjà vu. Another stranger emerged from the crowd, and began to head directly towards the trash can holding the folder. There was one major difference between the previous mystery figure, and the current person heading to the receptacle. The new suspect did not even try to hide their identity, and they were in a dead sprint towards the trash can. Before Asadi's brain could react, the girl reached in, grabbed the folder and took off in a dead sprint. To his complete surprise, Asadi recognized the sprinting girl. Even more surprising to him was that the fleeing girl was Abigail Crenna. *"What would Abigail want with this folder, and what has she gotten herself into?"* Asadi asked himself as he began chasing her through the streets. He wondered why she wanted it, but more importantly how had she known it was there? She was only 19 years old, so youth was on her side in this foot race. Abigail seemed to be slowing, when he noticed a slight limp. This was in his favor, but at this point her youth was still keeping her well in the lead. Abigail weaved between buildings, and rounded the back corner of an empty store that was located next to Randy's computer repair shop. When Asadi reached the same corner, Abigail was nowhere in sight. It seemed like she had vanished into thin air.

Logan needed to have background noise while setting up his equipment. Sheriff's headquarters had a TV that was set up in the room he was using. He turned the TV on and tuned it to WFIX news, which provided background sounds. Now that his equipment was set up and ready to go, Logan had become enthralled in what the news was showing around the country. Chaos and mayhem appeared to be escalating to violence in major cities all across America.

One of the live videos on the news showed police cars, dumpsters and buildings being set on fire. People ran indiscriminately through the streets throwing rocks, pieces of wood, and anything they could find at the police who were attempting to bring control to all this rioting. The live camera panned to a row of stores with a group of looters using hammers, or other tools, to break the store windows and doors. The looters entered the retail buildings through the now broken windows. They grabbed as much merchandise as they could carry. Another camera focused on the flow of fully stocked looters exiting the stores through more broken windows. The recent culture of nationwide police demoralization from public mistrust had created reluctance in the men and women in blue. They were hesitant to do anything to help eliminate this surge in criminal activity. Logan was surprised, appalled, and angered by what he was now witnessing on the TV screen.

Another news video broadcasted live feed of another city that had been declared an autonomous zone. The citizens within this lawless zone were shown standing on top of police cars with bull horns declaring their freedom from local and federal authorities. The area was walled off by cement barriers, cars, trucks, and anything the people of this new zone within America could find. In public, politicians were fighting to end these protests peacefully, while in the background they were actually authorizing this ignorance. The people within the zone were becoming more and more brazen. Inside the zone, makeshift housing lined the sidewalks. The people refused to dismantle their new territory, or their cause, until the American government provided them the income they felt was justly owed.

Another TV network showed the new national epidemic called the "smash-n-grab." The reporter explained that large crowds would stampede into a store and begin smashing things. Then the crowd would grab as many items as they could carry, and then walk back out into the street with the merchandise they now "owned." Their arms fully loaded, they would hit the street and leave freely without repercussion. Security guards and police were helpless to respond due to the new snowflake attitude on crime and Herculean reaction toward any type of police activity. This was a new phenomenon in America that many people viewed as looting, but there was one major difference. "Smash-n-grabs" were organized before they happened. Looting, on the other hand, was a spontaneous reaction by a group of angry people who had taken to the streets for a common cause, and an irrational violent atmosphere ensued.

Logan noted this was not happening in just one or two cities; it was happening all over America. Government authorities would not appear on TV news to communicate the need for calm across the nation. They were cowering to the revolutionaries. Officials allowed these causes to prosper and become more and more violent and hysterical.

Abigail ran bursting into the back room of the computer repair shop. She ran through the programming room, and into the larger conference room where Boris, Mikhail and Randy were meeting. Abigail came through the open door, slammed it, shut and threw the folder onto the long table so it landed in front of Boris. Abigail pulled her pistol, pointed it at her brother's head and began talking in a very nervous and loud voice.

"Boris, this son of a bitch just left this folder for the Sheriff. He was lurking around, waiting for the Sheriff's department to arrive at the forestry building to deal with the chaos going on outside. I saw him clandestinely leave that folder in the trash can while the Sheriff's deputy watched. It smells of collusion, so let's just kill the traitor here and now!"

"Hold on a minute Abigail. Let's see what's in the folder before you overreact and kill another member of your family," replied Boris.

Boris opened the folder, and to his surprise, dismay and anger, it contained all the details of their plan to bring America to the brink of disaster. It also provided a detailed description of how to hack into Randy's system and put an end to their evil, viral program that they had used to infect the government system.

"Randy, you are a dead man, and now it is just a question as to when and who will kill you. You and your father were always the weakest links of this group. Your exceptional coding skill was the only reason that we have kept you alive up to now!" exclaimed Boris.

"I killed my father and his little EMT tart, and it would give me great pleasure to kill his only son," screamed Abigail as she eased her finger onto the trigger.

"Not here and not yet, you little twit! There will be no more killing until I explain the recent developments to my superiors. You have all made a mess of this situation, and I have every reason to believe your sloppy behavior has already alerted the wrong people to what has been going on here. You kidnapped a baby, killed the primary author of this entire endeavor, and then you kidnapped his wife. And to top it all off, you really believe with these high level crimes that your secrets are safe. You are imbeciles and both may soon be dead," Mikhail shouted.

CHAPTER 29

Jack continued to examine the area where he had found the suspect tire tracks. He did not want to venture down the road without Zach and Red being there as his backup. Jack had just found something that was glistening in the sunlight, and it stuck out of one of the small piles of dirt created by the sliding tires. Jack thought it looked like a piece of glass from a broken light bulb in a car's tail or brake light system. It was significant in that it was another sign that a car with damage may have been in the area. Red and Zach arrived, skidded in the soft dirt, and pulled in next to Jack's vehicle. After the dust had settled, they jumped out of the car.

"Hi Jack, what have you found for us?" asked Red immediately after getting out of the car.

Jack showed them the suspect tire tracks and glass that he had found. Immediately after examining the clues, they all piled into

Red's car, and slowly began their journey back down the dirt road looking for additional clues.

"Boris, did your man, the one who kidnapped the baby, set the explosive that would completely destroy the squad car he had stolen? I have no idea if there was evidence in that car, which is why he was told to make sure it was destroyed," Ivan asked over the phone.

"He was told to do so. If he did as we had asked, the explosion should happen soon. I have no way to confirm with him now, as you had the man executed," replied Boris with sarcasm.

"Your insolence grows daily, so remember what I told you; watch your back!" Ivan threatened menacingly.

"You have been killing your own men! You are the one who wanted Mikhail here, and you really have no idea what he is capable of doing. You think he works for you, so I would suggest you watch your own back," replied Boris.

Red followed the tracks of the wounded vehicle down the dirt road, and that led them deeper into the woods. Suddenly the tracks turned down another rock infested, bumpy backwoods road and Red turned to continue to stay with the clues.

"There is a clearing coming up," Zach shouted.

The car rounded a slight bend, and the woods began to clear on both sides of the road. An open field of grass, weeds, wildflowers, and a banged up squad car made up the view in this vast clearing. The mangled squad car was not hidden, but rather it appeared as if it had been hastily parked at the edge of the field. Red parked the car; the three men drew their guns and cautiously got out of the car. Red, Zach and Jack separated and slowly walked towards the squad car. It was doubtful that anyone was still in or near the car, but at this point they were not taking any chances. Without warning, the car suddenly exploded. Car parts flew in every direction. The force of the explosion jettisoned each man into the air with the hard ground providing a very rough landing. They were lucky to be alive, and knew if they had arrived seconds earlier, all of them may surely be dead. Red rolled over to upright himself when he came face to face with Elmear's favorite stuffed teddy bear. A glimpse of Elmear holding her small, soft white teddy bear friend flashed vividly in his mind. The bear was now charred and tattered, but in this time of crisis, it still brought a smile to Red's face. It gave him even greater resolve, and hope, that his daughter was alive and that they would find her soon.

"Is everyone ok?" Red yelled.

"A few bumps and bruises, but fine, considering what just happened," replied Zach.

"I'm good, but have some shrapnel in my arm. It's not too bad, so if one of you will just pull the piece of metal out and wrap it for me, we can keep moving," answered Jack weakly.

Red pulled the metal out of Jack's arm and finished wrapping the small wound with a bandage he retrieved from the trunk of his car. Any evidence that might have been in the car was now gone, but they did search the entire area just to be sure. Zach came across something interesting as he wandered deeper into the field.

"Guys come here," he yelled excitedly.

Red and Jack ran to Zach's position, and they were astonished by what they saw.

"This looks to me like a helicopter landed and then took off from this position. Look at the bent, folded vegetation all around this circular area. A small chopper must have been here," Zach explained.

"What does all of this mean? Does it mean they took Elmear far away from here? Does it mean they used the chopper for a quick move to a local area? They had to be flying low through clearings or someone would have noticed a helicopter. It is simply not an everyday occurrence to see a chopper flying around these woods," Red stated in a worried and confused voice.

"Let's follow this clearing, and maybe we will be able to determine the flight path," suggested Jack.

The three started their journey deeper into the wilderness in high hopes that they could determine what direction the kidnappers had fled. As he walked through the grass, Red could not let go of Elmear's favorite bear, praying that this was a powerful, positive sign that they would find her alive.

CHAPTER 30

Lily had not grown up in the little town of Crenna, nor was she the same person that everyone thought she was. Many years ago, Lily came to town as a bright-eyed recent college graduate of a prestigious business institution. Paul Crenna's father had hired her after an interview at a job fair from the college she had attended. Crenna wanted new and younger talent to make sure his logging office progressed, while keeping up with technology in America. During the interview, he found Lily to be very outgoing, pretty, exceptionally bright, pretty, numbers oriented, pretty, technologically savvy, obsessively organized, and last but not least, very sexy. He had an eye for beauty.

College was just another step in Lily's unique life that was wrought with continuous intense structured learning. Her life had not been that of a typical American child. Lily's fifteen-year old mother was forced to give her up to an orphanage so she could be adopted.

Lily's mother felt adoption would give her daughter a chance for a better life than she could ever provide. The orphanage Lily had been placed in was not a usual orphanage. The organization had no intention of ever putting any of the children up for adoption, unless they deemed the child incapable of following their stringent curriculum.

This was one of many such institutions around the world that was designed to optimize highly trained individuals. The children in these facilities went through rigorous training to build intense mental and physical toughness. The institution had to be sure that the young adults could endure any situation they were confronted with in American society outside of the orphanage. They were taught English, Russian, Chinese and Arabic languages. In addition, they had to learn each various country's history and culture which allowed them to blend into any sector of American society. The physical training and education was ongoing. The children trained seven days a week, three-hundred sixty-five days a year.

Lily graduated top of her class, and was considered a major success.

The world is full of deep dark secrets, but none as deep and dark as those who really rule over the American way of life. The people who had educated and trained Lily were the very same people who secretly control America. It's quite conceivable, and scary, to believe that similar, secret groups with different ideologies control Russia, China, and all other major countries in the world. The orphanages run by this secret group in America were vital to maintaining a constant level of highly trained people who are committed to the stability of the American way of life.

The American way of life was controlled and funded by a small sub-section of the government, and only a select few were privy to its existence. Interestingly enough, the select few did not include the President! This clandestine group's current goal was the pursuit of the reformation of a Republic America, rather than a swamp-filled Democracy. America's current population argued that America was already a Republic form of government. Money continually allowed rich politicians to swindle the American people into accepting that their beliefs were best for America; that is not how a Republic operates. This money allowed these scam artists to become career politicians, also not the intent of a Republic. A

Democracy that allowed foreign governments to influence its politicians would never occur in a Republic. This small controlling organization had been kept secretive throughout time, because the American public would not believe or comprehend what their government had become behind the scenes.

    At any point in time, the orphanage graduates could be called upon to aid in this push to change America. They would serve the cause no matter the personal cost, up to and including death. When these young adults were of age, and fully trained, their placement in society was at random until they were needed. With Paul Crenna's offer of a job, the powers that be allowed Lily to accept the job, become a member of society, and await instructions to fulfill her service. Lily settled into her life and job, and as fate would have it through an office love affair, she became infatuated with the son of the man who hired her, Paul Crenna. It was such a normal fulfilling life, at least for awhile. They had two children and Lily loved her family life. As their children grew, her husband Paul's real personality came through. He became verbally abusive to Lily, and was quite the "man about town." Lily had become emotionally involved, which was not supposed to have occurred in her line of work.

In addition to Paul's change in personality, Lily got the call she had been trained to take. This was an indication of how far-reaching the organization was who had trained Lily. They were completely aware of Paul Crenna's feelings towards America and would secretly align themselves with Crenna's cause. They knew what Paul had planned and would take steps to ensure that his plan was successful.

The organization decided to move in and take steps to make Paul's plan successful. The discovery that this secret American organization's Russian counterpart had become involved placed a higher level of importance to them while assisting Paul. They would ensure American news outlets labeled the correct government as the cause; make sure all collateral people involved from Russia were eliminated when the process was completed; and, last but not least, make sure Lily was still committed to their cause so she could be relocated and used in the future.

Up until now, Lily's only involvement had been information based. She was brought up to speed regarding all the players and the process. A second asset, Mikhail had been sent in to assist if necessary.

Alannah's attempted murder and Elmear's kidnapping were not part of the equation, so now Lily must utilize her talents to prevent these innocents from being harmed.

CHAPTER 31

Boris Mertvago came to Crenna with the knowledge that he would be placed there for a long period of time. He had rented a beautiful farmhouse in the middle of nowhere, a good distance from the town of Crenna. The farm sat in the middle of a vast field that had about a quarter of a mile of wooded frontage between it and the main road. The driveway to the house was a quarter of a mile long, and it was an enchanting drive through that area's bountiful forest. There were times when Boris would stop midway down the driveway, get out of his car, light his cigar and just bask in the quiet beauty of this forest near his home base. This big tough killer loved the calming effect that nature brought to his soul. Boris's life was spent in a facility whose mission was to teach young people to become Russian operatives. These operatives' lifelong path was to support the few people that secretly controlled Russia. Most of the world hated Putin for leading Russia with brutality, but Putin was only the pawn. He was a pawn to these powerful men who put him in place to be the face of their agenda, and take the brunt of the world's contempt.

Originally, Boris wanted the solitude of the farmhouse to be able to escape the daily stress of being forced to take on the role of Ivan's right-hand man. He would have killed Ivan long ago, but out of necessity his superiors had prevented this from happening. Boris's reasoning for this farmhouse solitude had recently changed, and in fact that reason was now coming up the long driveway.

The car was speeding up the dirt road leaving a large cloud of dust behind. The vehicle skidded to a stop in front of his house. The driver side door opened, and a beautiful, young girl stepped out of the vehicle and ran to Boris. She jumped into his arms and held on for dear life. This had been an unexpected love affair for Boris. He was twenty years this girl's senior, and could not imagine why this young, vibrant girl desired his affection. He didn't care what the reason was; he loved the peace and joy she brought to his turbulent life.

"Miss Abigail Crenna, what brings you to this neck of the woods?" Boris asks coyly.

"I heard some big oaf living in this remote location was in need of some company, and I wanted to help my fellow man. So I decided to drive out and see if I could help!" Abigail replied coyly.

Their playful verbal banter quickly turned physical, and they went into the house to continue their love making indoors. Boris was eager to bask in this young woman's desires, but his training kept him from fully trusting Abigail. He knew full well her affections may have been led by ulterior motives to thwart his own group's plan.

Phase one of the expansive scheme to break down American society was well under way. It was now time for phase two to get started. Depending on its success, this could very well be the final phase. They had to monitor America's atmosphere closely, because if the chaos went too far, society would reach the point of no return.

Boris could not depend on Randy, even though he was under heavy guard. He could easily sabotage phase two without the guards ever knowing.

"Unfortunately, I have to get back to the repair shop Abigail. Maybe we could see each other later when I am sure everything is running smooth at the shop," Boris said.

"Isn't it about time people knew that we are a couple? What's the big deal? Let's get dressed, and I will ride with you into town," replied Abigail.

"No! You really have no idea the repercussions I face if my employers discover our relationship! Mikhail already has you on his radar because of what you heard when you burst into the office with that folder. We don't need to give him any more to think about, or any more reason for him to mistrust me. You will go your way, and I will go my way today. Our relationship will remain our secret! Do you understand?" asked Boris.

"Not really. I don't give a rat's ass what your so called 'superiors' think! Haven't I proven my loyalty to you, and to whatever you and your playmates are doing? I killed my father, and am ready to kill my brother whenever you give the word. You need to loosen up a little lover!" Abigail quipped.

Boris's face turned beet red, he grabbed her arm and began yelling in her face. "Listen, you spoiled little brat. You killed your father for your own reasons that are no concern of ours. You are a violent little bitch that I will never completely trust. Today you have made a grave mistake, because you will not leave this house, and in fact you may never leave."

Boris dragged Abigail by the arm into the barn. He made her sit on the dirty hay-strewn floor just in front of a metal animal stall so he could figure out where to keep her until he returned later that evening. He realized the barn must have been used for auto repairs at some point in time. There was a hinged wooden door over a cement pit in the floor that was used to work underneath a vehicle. Boris pulled open the door, grabbed Abigail and forced her into the cement pit. He lowered the door, temporarily placing a few heavy blocks on top. Boris then ran outside, and jumped into Abigail's car. She had never removed her keys, so he started the engine and drove it into the garage over the pit to secure the door until he returned. This would not only keep her hidden, but would also keep her car out of sight. Boris closed the barn door, and returned to the house to get ready to leave for town.

Once he had pulled himself together, Boris got into his own car and began the long ride to the repair shop. Phase two was the interruption of American power grids, and when they shut down it would disrupt every aspect of American life.

CHAPTER 32

As the three men continued to walk the clearing where the squad car had exploded, the vast openness started to close in on them with woods on both sides. It reminded Red of an airplane runway that was lined by majestic old trees, and greenery on both sides. This natural runway suddenly ended at an open corridor, which spanned to the left and to the right, as far as the eye could see.

"This has to be the flight path of the helicopter, and it fits into what happened the other night. If you head up the corridor to the right, you can get to the Southern logging office. This is where Paul Crenna died, and we were attacked by a helicopter. The helicopter was armed with men hanging out on both sides who strafed the entire area with machine guns. I agree, this corridor would be the perfect flight path for a chopper to attack and escape the area," explained Red.

"I've got my cell phone with me, so you two continue searching by car and I will walk the corridor to the left. I know the reception here is spotty, but you will still be able to track me sporadically," Zach stated.

"Let me do that Zach. I know my way around the area a little better. You go with Jack and search by car," suggested Red.

"No Red. You need to be readily available if Alannah or the town needs you. Also, what if you get a tip on Elmear's location, and you are in the middle of nowhere? You need to be ready to move on a moment's notice. I'll walk the corridor and keep in touch with you as my cell phone reception allows," replied Zach.

Red knew Zach was correct so he made sure Zach was armed with a few spare clips for his pistol. Zach began his hike in the wilderness, while Red and Jack headed back on the dirt road in the car. They made their way back to the main road, and slowly headed in the same direction as Zach's hike would take him. They came to another logger's road and decided to venture back into the woods as far into the wilderness as this forest highway would take them. There were roads like this all through the area. It was a logger's paradise and these so-called "roads" were their lifeline to extracting the wooded bounty out for public use. Clearings popped up here and there as they traveled deeper into the forest. All of a sudden, something metal glistening in the sun coming through the trees, caught Jack's eye.

"Red, continue driving until you round that next corner! Stop the car when we are out of sight of anyone who might be near that clearing. I saw something metal back in that thick pine grove. I have no idea how big or what it might be, but it's worth checking out," explained Jack.

Red did as Jack asked. They exited the car, left it running to avoid suspicion, and then quietly shut the doors to avoid the car's door open alarm from sounding. Guns drawn, the two men crept their way back to the pine grove to see what Jack had seen nestled in the many evergreen trees.

Zach was trying to remain alert, but found it difficult as he walked through the wondrous calming mountain scenery. He noticed much of the high greenery was bent in many directions which could be the result of a low flying helicopter. The corridor now took a left hand turn, and the telltale bend in the high grass continued to be evident. This leg of the corridor ended when Zach reached a remote body of water. He began walking the perimeter of the small lake, hopeful he would find a dwelling. This was the perfect location for a quintessential mountain cabin built for hunting, trapping or even vacations.

As Red and Jack rounded the corner in the road, they decided to stay in the woods and circle to the area where Jack had caught a glimpse of the metal. There was a small clearing ahead of the pine grove, but they wanted to avoid being out in the open until they knew what or whom they were dealing with. It was very slow going as the deeper the two got into the thick evergreens the more difficult it was to move around. Suddenly, they both saw their destination, a large tractor trailer hidden among the many evergreen trees. This was not just a trailer, but rather the entire rig, cab and all! The two men continued their cautious journey towards the truck. When they got close enough to realize there was no one in or around the truck, they moved in for a closer inspection. Jack climbed into the cab to inspect the inside for any clues.

"Nothing out of the ordinary and I don't find any ke …," Jack did not finish his sentence because as he lifted the floor mat, he found something hidden under the rubber mat. "Scratch that thought.

I just found a set of keys under the driver side floor mat," Jack told Red.

Jack put the keys he had found into the ignition and, sure enough, the truck started right away. They decided to pull it out into the clearing so that they could inspect it under less cramped conditions. Once in a more open location, Jack turned off the engine and removed the keys to see if one of them would unlock the large trailer doors. Luck was not with them as none of the keys fit the door locking mechanism.

"We don't have time to mess around," Red said as he ran to his running car they had left around the corner on the dirt road. Once inside the car, he put it in reverse, and moved the rear end of the car within six feet of the trailer. Red opened the trunk and removed a large chain with tow hooks on both ends. He hooked one end to the lower frame of the car, while Jack hooked the other end to the trailer doors. Red got into the driver seat, moved the car forward to take up some of the slack in the chain, and then floored the gas pedal. The force pulled the locking mechanism off the door and both doors swung open. Red jumped out of the car to see if there had been anything in the trailer. Jack and Red stood at the end of the trailer speechless for a few moments. Their minds had to catch up to what their eyes were seeing inside the trailer that had been abandoned in the wilderness.

Zach continued moving through the thick brush along the edge of the lake, when he suddenly caught a whiff of the distinct odor of cigarette smoke. He stopped and crouched into the brush, watching and listening to the sounds around him. Through the brush he saw the cigarette smoke swirl into the air, and now that he had stopped moving through the loud dry forest, Zach could hear voices off in the distance. The voices soon stopped and he heard a door slam shut. Zach stood and began to slowly move in the direction that he had heard the voices. As he reached the crest of a small hill, Zach could see a large log cabin built amongst the forest, lining the lake. It was not the cabin that necessarily caught his eye, but rather it was the large professional looking black SUV parked near the cabin. This was not your typical hunting or family vacation vehicle. The next sound he heard filled Zach with hope, and got his heart racing with nervous excitement. He had to carefully leave the area, and contact Red as quickly as possible.

CHAPTER 33

Abigail was now in a crazed state of anger over being holed up in an old automotive repair pit beneath the barn floor. She turned on her cell phone's flashlight to look for a way out, and began talking to herself.

"And you have no idea who YOU are dealing with Boris, you sissy little bitch. I can't believe I slept with your old, wrinkly ass, just to get more details on my scumbag father's master plan, and what part Randy played in the entire scheme."

She continued mumbling and grumbling until the sight of an old wooden sledgehammer brought a smile to her face. She thought maybe with this tool, she could break through the center of the door above her, where there was no weight from the car. It sounded good, but Abigail also knew her escape would depend on the positioning of the parked the car above her. Plus, there was always the distinct possibility that her demolition would weaken the structure above her, causing the car to fall into the pit.

Abigail started swinging the heavy tool using the rush of adrenaline created from her continued rage, which had provided her abnormal strength. She swung yelling, "Ughhhhhhh, take that Mr. Small!" which was the nickname she had given Boris for various mental and physical reasons.

The first and second swings of the hammer weakened the area it struck. The continued hits eventually created a hole in the door above her that was covering the pit. Abigail had stuck the hammer through the hole, and turned it to lock it in place. She then pulled with all her strength using the head of the sledgehammer as a pry bar. It worked because some the slats that the door was made up of pulled free and fell to the floor of the pit, just missing her head. Abigail now had a potential escape route if she could pull herself through the hole, and if the car was positioned to allow her a short path to crawl from under the car. She used the phone flashlight once again, and located an old round oil drum. Abigail moved the drum to center in under the hole above. Hoisting herself onto the top of the drum, she was then able to squeeze through the hole, and slide right under the rear end of the car to freedom.

"Nice job Borass! Your shoddy driving skills left me plenty of room to escape," Abigail said out loud.

She got into her car and brought the engine to life.

"Borass, you must have been in panic mode because you also left the keys in the ignition. You are truly a real genius!" Abigail quipped to herself as she put the car into drive and drove through the back wall of the barn. Boards, hay and farm implements flew everywhere, but she didn't care. Once outside, Abigail slammed on the brakes putting the car into a sliding stop. She took stock of her weapon hidden inside the car, along with the ammunition.

Abigail sped down the long driveway away from the farmhouse and headed for Crenna. Today's quest in town would ultimately be for revenge.

A group of Americans heading the small, but powerful organization trying to change America's direction had gathered to outline in awe the many concerns operating in the small mountain town of Crenna! The concern was that these various groups could collide at any time and bring their vision crumbling down. The few times they had met in the past, the members always took a little time for levity. People were always theorizing of their existence and coming up with names for the group. The newest subversive name floating around America was the ominous sounding, "Deep State." In reality they had no group name, because naming them would provide another path to be able to research their existence.

Now down to the serious business at hand, Calian Nakai began outlining the status of the situation in Crenna, which would hopefully provide the group the information needed to make any necessary course corrections.

"We have our own operatives continuing their work inside Crenna. Lily Crenna and Mikhail are working to secure the area to prevent the death of any more innocents. The two know of each other, but to date have had no contact. Lily is currently in a tense situation in captivity knowing she must save a baby the Russians plan to remove from America.

"Our Russian counterpart organization has found a way to incorporate their violent ideology into our plan to break down America. This has the potential of bringing our country to the point of no return. The players they have embedded into this town are Ivan

Vladmelov, his wife during this exercise Svetlana Vladmelov, and Boris Mertvago. Boris was the key player in their very successful 'Russian Disinformation' campaign last year. They have also brought a contingent of soldiers, along with various pieces of Russian equipment such as a helicopter."

"Then there is the exceptionally capable local Sheriff's office working on many fronts. Liam (Red) Kelly and Asadi Zawar make up the entire Sheriff's department. Red has brought in a group of well trained military friends to aid him in finding his daughter, the baby in captivity with Lily. This group is also working to control the area, and has had encounters with Ivan's Russian soldiers. Unfortunately, these men were unknowingly involved in the death of one of our men. Boris sent Mikhail to kill the three Russian prisoners. We countered those orders to have Mikhail remove the prisoners from the jail, then place them into hiding and create a story to convince Boris that they were gone forever. Mayhem ensued, leaving Mikhail's organization no choice but to kill Ivan's men. In the heat of the battle, Red's people killed one of Mikhail's operatives. This is when we knew the lines were getting cloudy and we had to do something.

"As an aside, I have worked closely with this group of American hero's. Red, his wife Alannah, Zach Morrelli, Layla Morrelli, Logan Wilson and Jack Miller were instrumental in saving America from the Chinese invasion on American soil. I know these people do not work directly for our organization, but they are just as capable, and loyal, if not more so than our own trained team."

"There are two unexpected villains: Abigail and Randy Crenna! Randy tried to opt out by contacting the CIA. He provided details of his father's plan, and the Russians' involvement, but his desire to help the CIA was in question. We stepped in to tell the CIA to stay out of this situation entirely. His sister Abigail has gone completely rogue, killing her father, and now seeking revenge for Randy's involvement. She went so far as to become intimately involved with Boris to gain information. We should alert Mikhail to keep a close eye on her activities and step in if necessary."

Calian Nakai had entered politics to help change America. He entered the political arena as a Senator, and had recently lost in his election run for President of this great land. His loyalty and commitment to change America had made him a top candidate to become a member of this elite group of Americans. Nakai suggested that they let this group of loyalists continue to handle the issues in their town. They should alert Lily and Mikhail that Red and his friends were on their side, and to stand down unless Red asked for their help. This clandestine group agreed with Nakai unanimously.

CHAPTER 34

Nakai reached out to Lily and Mikhail with the new directives. Mikhail would be contacted by phone, because he was still able to move freely about town. Lily was still a captive inside the cabin, so her chip would need to be utilized. This elite organization took advantage of every technological discovery that would assist them in their efforts. This unique chip was implanted in the operative's ear canal so it could never be detected. If normal methods of communication were not possible, they could broadcast a message to their teams using this chip. Lily received the instructions, but at this point her options were limited. Ivan decided that simply locking her in a room was not secure enough. The room he chose had no windows, and he left his only remaining armed guard outside the door. Lily would have to bide her time, and wait for an opportune moment to strike back to help Elmear.

"Has phase two been initiated," Ivan asked Boris over the phone.

"Power grids that supply New York City, Los Angeles, Chicago, St. Louis, New Orleans and Savannah are now in disaster recovery mode. It's only been a short time, but as days with no power add up, the public will become increasingly less patient than they are now. As anticipated, someone in the government has finally realized that they are no longer in control of the computer system. Our main focus for our programming team now is to be sure we maintain control of their computer for as long as possible. Unbeknownst to you, my superiors also told me to unleash part of phase three as an insurance policy. We have hit multiple food processing plants with fires, planes crashing into buildings, and the power outages I stated earlier. Also, the re-introduction of the bird flu will severely impact America's food processing, creating meat shortages everywhere," Boris explained and added, "and inflation will rise exponentially."

"Stay in touch and let me know immediately if anything changes," demanded Ivan, which he said deceitfully. He was done with this project, and his only concern was to get out of the country.

Ivan ordered his driver to load the car because they were leaving this town.

"Put the new car seat in first so we can get our baby settled," added Svetlana.

Ivan walked by the guard outside Lily's room, and stopped to give him instructions. "After we leave kill her, then rendezvous with Boris. The two of you get the hell out of this godforsaken country, and meet me at our home in Sardinia." He wanted Boris to escape to his home in Sardinia just so he could kill him. Boris's loyalties had changed, and that had not sat well with Ivan!

Lily heard her fate as she listened for activity outside her prison door. This would be her only opportunity to overtake the guard. Right now, she could only hope that this would not be too late for her to free Elmear from her captors.

Svetlana went outside with Elmear, and carefully placed her into the car seat. The car was now loaded with everything they had decided to take, which was very little. Ivan and Svetlana left the cabin, and were now inside the car ready to go. Ivan's driver closed all car doors, positioned himself in the driver's seat, and started driving the vehicle through the rough terrain towards the main road.

"I am so excited to get home and show our baby Anastasia her new room," Svetlana said to Ivan kissing him on the cheek.

When the guard heard the car start, he unlocked the room holding Lily. *"This must have been one of Ivan's challenged guards,"* Lily remembers thinking to herself when the guard opened the door as if he were entering an empty room. His face was met with the round metal base that kept a floor lamp upright. Lily was holding the lamp pole as a weapon, and had rammed the base into the guards face knocking him to the floor. She pounced on him, grabbing his pistol before he could re-group after this blow to the face.

Rather than kill him, Lily knocked the man out with the butt of the gun. She grabbed the handcuffs on his person and, as an added measure, cuffed him to a metal water pipe coming up through the floor. She also locked the door behind her, and quickly went outside to see if Ivan's car was still in sight.

The car was gone, but before she could devise a plan she heard the roar of a truck coming towards the cabin. The sound was coming from the forest on the other side of the small lake. She caught a glimpse of a tractor trailer cab driving through the brush bouncing off small trees. The truck began to round the lake never letting off the gas. The abuse this truck was incurring gave Lily the feeling it would never make it to the cabin. She found a hidden place to observe the oncoming vehicle, and hopefully would find help from whoever was inside!

CHAPTER 35

Abigail was handling the country road leading to Crenna like an experienced Grand Prix driver. She sped to the inner edge of each corner without any thought of decreasing her speed, than banked to the outer edge of the next corner. The only two things on this young girl's mind were named "Boris" and "Randy". She wanted one, if not both of these men dead. Randy's fate would depend on how deeply he was involved with the Russians.

Recently, something inside Abigail had snapped. Her ability to reason through conflict with rational methods had disappeared. Her ability to feel compassion was gone. The mental illness thread within her family tree may have come home to roost.

Abe Crenna's wife had a history of irrational behavior. In today's medical world, her behavior would have been diagnosed as mental illness, and she would have been treated with medication. In her time, she was treated with isolation, scorn and homemade elixirs, none of which helped her. While the townspeople thought her sudden death was suspicious, no one had pursued investigating the circumstances. So now it seemed that Abigail was carrying on this family trait as she was headed towards certain disaster.

With the town in sight, the highway speed limit signs indicated a reduction in speed, which Abigail ignored! Prior to this, the danger was only to her, but now as she raced through the streets of Crenna, she began endangering others. Abigail's end game was almost in sight. She was now only blocks away from the computer repair shop. Her eyes wide, her breathing increased, and her foot pressed the gas pedal even closer to the floor as she drove manically towards her target.

The shop was adorned with a large picture window in the front. This picture window was in the direct path of the store's counter area, which was in front of the wall that separated the storefront from the back of the building. Abigail bounced over the curb of the parking lot, took out a few signs, and sped toward the picture window. The car slowed slightly only when it clipped another vehicle partially parked in its path. Luckily the store clerk was gazing out the window during a slow sales period, and was able to jump out of the way to safety.

Abigail steered the car through the window, into the store's solid wooden counter, through the back wall and into the office area. People were screaming as they scurried around to safety. The front of the car was sticking through the wall into an open hallway between offices, while the wall itself crumbled onto the roof of the car. Abigail made it through the crash alive, but not unscathed. Her face was bloodied and a narrow piece of molding came through the windshield and entered her body just below her left shoulder. Without any cry of pain she snapped the molding with her right hand which would allow her to move more freely.

Boris unearthed himself from the rubble and tried to maneuver his body to stand. Abigail saw him out of her driver side window. It was only at this moment that she realized that she really had not made it through this crash. She looked down and saw a pool of blood that was rushing from her left wrist that had been slit by a piece of the windshield when it shattered. Her vision was beginning to blur, and she was on the verge of passing out just before death took hold. Her last act was to raise her pistol and pull the trigger multiple times in Boris's direction until her consciousness faded to black.

Abigail had been successful in achieving part of her mission. All three of her gunshots had struck Boris, and his dead body fell back into the rubble. Randy was in his office on the left hand side of where the car had come through the wall. He was unharmed because that area of the building had remained somewhat intact. Randy saw that his sister was dead, and grief came over him. His mother and sister were all he had left, and while he knew his sister hated him of late, he still held hope that would change in the future. Now there was no hope of re-connecting with her, and his mother was missing, and he had no idea where she had gone. As Randy surveyed the scene he noticed Boris was also dead, and it was then he realized he had to pull it together, and help make things right.

Randy went into the programming area and told everyone to leave the building. No one was hurt, but most of them were in hiding or had already gone outside.

"We are done here! Leave and don't come back. Your life is now yours, and if you are questioned about what went on here; tell the truth!" Randy yelled inside and then went outside and repeated the same message.

After clearing the building, Randy went about destroying every piece of computer equipment in the building to assure the end of their group's cyberattack on America. He had very little time to accomplish this, because he could already hear the sounds of fire and emergency personnel vehicles headed in his direction. Randy knew he would ultimately pay for his acts against America, and he was ok with that. It was time to end this and accept the consequences for his mistakes.

CHAPTER 36

"Red, this is Zach. I followed the corridor which eventually led me to a small lake. I started to search around the lake, and have found a cabin. You need to get over here as quickly as possible. In front of the cabin there was a black SUV, but what's more important is what I heard. The distinct sounds of a crying baby were emanating from inside the cabin. There was no recreational gear outside the cabin; no fireplace, no grill, no bikes, no boat, nothing giving the appearance of a family vacation. That, plus the black SUV with tinted windows gave me cause to be concerned. I made my way back to the corridor so that I could call you, and please hurry to my location," explained Zach.

"We'll be right there Zach. Hang tight!" replied Red.

Red quickly explained the situation to Jack, who immediately jumped into action and began disconnecting the truck from its trailer. Red jumped inside the trailer, and started cutting every wire and hose he could find to prevent the helicopter from being accessed. Jack got into the cab, started the engine and waited anxiously for Red.

Red climbed into the cab, and the two men headed out to the main road. They were going back to the end of the first logging road where they had left Zach. When they reached the main road they had to wait for a black SUV and five other vehicles to pass before they could leave the dirt road. Red was growing impatient while they waited for this unusual traffic to pass by them. He was so overcome with anxiety he could barely focus. Once on the main road, Jack pushed the massive truck to its limits, and soon they were racing down the original logging road. The rig was not meant to be an off road racing vehicle, and was taking a beating. Red and Jack were also being thrown from side to side inside the truck's cab. They reached the corridor, and headed out onto the field towards Zach. At times the truck actually left the ground, and then landed with brutal force. Red and Jack continued to take a beating, but moved forward undeterred. As they veered with the bend of the open corridor, they saw Zach standing at the edge of the woods. Jack stopped the truck giving Zach time to jump onto the passenger side running board to speak to Red.

"Red, we should go on foot from here so we can approach the cabin …" Red interrupted Zach, "I can't Zach. We wasted way too much time already driving through the woods, because I didn't know what road to take to the cabin. Hold on to the steel grab bar Zach. We can get there much quicker in the truck."

All three readied their weapons and Jack pressed the gas pedal to the floor. The truck moved through the trees bending the heavy brush while bouncing from side to side. As they approached the water, Jack steered the truck on the path along the lakeside. It wasn't long before Zach had to jump off or risk being thrown by the force of the bouncing truck. Had Red listened to Zach he would have realized the truck was actually slowing them down due to the terrain, and was actually making an exceptional amount of noise. This became evident as Red watched Zach run ahead of them, turn and aim his pistol at him. Jack knew what Zach was doing and he slammed on the breaks bringing the truck to a sudden stop.

Red slammed his fists onto the dash yelling, "What in the hell are you doing. My daughter is in trouble and you decide to point a gun at me?"

"Shut up and get out of the truck you stubborn fool!" yelled Zach.

While Red exited the rig, Zach holstered his pistol, sprinted towards Red slamming him to the ground.

Zach jumped on top of Red, and was nose to nose when he spoke softly but forcefully, "You are acting like a newbie. I know it's your daughter, but if you go in there like a madman you will get her and yourself killed. Plus you don't even know who is in that cabin. We do this like the soldiers we are, so you get yourself right and let's do this."

Jack stood cover with his pistol, and let the situation play out.

"I'm good Zach. You are right and I will follow your lead, my friend."

From her hiding place, Lily was watching the truck battle its way through the woods, and then saw it stop. She could see men get out of the truck, but then she lost sight of them.

Zach, Red and Jack split up to approach the cabin from different angles, and began moving in stealth fashion through the woods. Zach saw her first, crouched under a clump of thick bushes that were bent over forming a small natural lean to. Zach pointed his weapon through the bushes that provided her cover and said, "Do not move. If you have a weapon, put it down, then lay flat to the ground and stay still."

"These guys are good! I never saw or heard them coming," Lily thought to herself as she followed Zach's instructions to the letter.

Zach was now in front of Lily and told her to sit up, but remain out of sight.

"Who are you and who is in the cabin," Zach asked her.

"My name is Lily Crenna. The only person left in the cabin is the guard I disabled. Everyone else, including Elmear, just left the cabin," replied Lily.

Zach told Lily to begin moving towards the cabin quietly. He told her to head to her left which is where he knew Red would be. Just before they were about to break through the woods in front of the cabin, Red saw Lily.

"Lily, what are you doing here?"

"Red, please listen carefully. Ivan and Svetlana just left here in a black SUV. They have Elmear. They are headed to their home in

Sardinia where they plan to raise Elmear as their own. To them, Elmear's name is now Anastasia Vladmelov," explained Lily.

"How do you know all this, and why should I believe you?" Red exploded.

By now, Zach realized the Black SUV he had seen parked outside was now gone.

Lily composed herself and replied, "I came here to get away, and was captured by Ivan and his group of thugs. My mission was recently altered, and I am to assist you in getting your baby back. Calian Nakai says I can trust you and your friends. I cannot explain any further. I have organized a quick departure to Sardinia, but you need to decide quickly what you want to do."

Just then Red turned pale, realizing that the black SUV they had seen on the main road earlier probably had had his baby inside.

"I'm yours! Let's go," Red replied with determination.

CHAPTER 37

Red called Asadi and asked him to release their one and only prisoner. Lily Crenna had provided one additional piece of information, which was that Mikhail was working with her, and the prisoner was one of Mikhail's men. At this point, she would provide no further details.

Asadi released the man and quickly assigned him to work in assisting with the growing chaos in Crenna.

Asadi decided it would be best to close the forestry office. People were still clamoring to get answers about their missing government funds. The only way to keep those workers safe was to seal the building until things were calmer.

Asadi found the scene at the computer repair shop very distressing. He had witnessed death and destruction in Afghanistan, but this should not be happening in his quiet little town. A beautiful young girl sat dead in her mangled car with a pierced shoulder, and blood pooled around her sliced wrist. Building debris was everywhere. The big Russian, who Asadi barely knew, lay dead on top of this debris with three bullet holes adorning his body.

"This is a horrific scene, but then again it is a miracle that more people were not killed," Asadi said to Logan.

Asadi knew Red was leaving town, so it was up to him to work through this mess and keep people safe. He had already contacted the State Police and coroner for additional help with the crime scene.

Randy had finished the destruction of all his computer systems, and walked back to the murder scene. He had come through the door to the office area; he carried the bat he used to destroy equipment, and looked like a crazed man with a weapon. Not knowing Randy's intentions, Asadi and Logan drew their weapons and pointed them at Randy.

"Stop right there Crenna! Drop the weapon, and put your hands behind your head," yelled Asadi.

Randy responded quickly, and Logan moved in to put him in handcuffs. While the coroner and State Police worked the scene, Asadi and Logan took Randy into his office, which was still somewhat intact. The information flowed from Randy's mouth as he was eager to unburden himself. As Asadi and Logan listened to the wild story unfold, both men knew the next step would be to involve the FBI.

All of a sudden, three strange men dressed in three-piece suits, swaggered into the debris area. The front man pulled a flat leather case from his inside suit coat pocket. As the man approached Asadi holding this case, it fell open to show his FBI badge and credentials.

"The FBI is taking this man into custody for crimes against the United States government. Your jurisdiction in this matter ends now," the man demanded in a very monotone, rude voice.

"I'm not so sure about that. While you may have jurisdiction over the crimes you say he committed, I have jurisdiction over the investigation into the two deaths that took place in this man's repair shop. Your fancy badge and threats mean little to me. Whatever happened to law enforcement working together? If you would like to change your tone, and attitude, then maybe we can work this out as two professionals!" replied Asadi with Logan smiling in the background.

The man turned and, with a nod from the man in the background, he moved aside while this third man walked towards Asadi. Logan placed his hand on the top of his pistol to ready himself for action.

"I am Agent Ward of the FBI and we do need your cooperation. This man has committed high crimes against his government, and has placed America in turmoil. I understand your need to question him about what happened here, so please continue with your investigation. We will wait as long as necessary, but we need to take this man into custody today."

"That works, and thank you for your understanding," replied Asadi.

Logan and Asadi went back to interrogating Randy who really had little definitive information as to why this death scene took place. He enlightened them on the possible affair between Boris and Abigail. He used the word possible; because he was not a hundred percent sure it was true. And even if it were true, he had no idea why his sister would create such a disaster and kill Boris. The main point of interest to Asadi was when Randy informed them that Abigail had admitted to killing their father over his actions against his country and against their mother. Along with this revelation was her threat to kill Randy as well. Again, no insight to her actions that day, but he did shed some light on her father's murder. Asadi knew Abigail to be a kind, driven young adult and found it difficult to believe she would do something like this if she was in her right mind. He had little knowledge of any mental illness in Abigail or her family. Asadi was satisfied for now, and told Agent Ward to take Randy away, but left the door open for them to ask further questions in the future.

    Asadi found the entire situation extremely worrisome. He pondered how the FBI could know of the situation in Crenna at the same time Randy was informing them of the details surrounding the computer hijacking. The answer to this would come out much later as Red worked to obtain additional information, and had expressed his working theory to Asadi in a private moment.

CHAPTER 38

Ivan, Svetlana and their beautiful little kidnapped baby Anastasia were comfortably flying in their private jet to the airport in Olbia on the island of Sardinia. The second largest island in the Mediterranean Sea, Sardinia was a destination for many Russian oligarchs. The world-renowned coastal region of northern Sardinia, referred to as the Emerald Coast, was one of the most expensive and beautiful in the world. Ivan Vladmelov had purchased a large, stately complex in the small coastal village of Portisco. This was their ultimate destination.

"I can't wait to show our daughter the beauty of Sardinia. I think we should raise her in the wondrous atmosphere that Sardinia offers, rather than a chaotic, stress-filled life in Russia. We can take her to Asinara on our yacht to show her the mysterious albino donkeys. Tomorrow, I want to take Anastasia to the jewelry store in Portisco to get her darling little ears pierced. Then we'll buy her a delicate little pair of Sardinian red coral earrings. I'm so excited about our new life, my love. Aren't you?" asked Svetlana.

"If this means we can remain a family, and you will curb your appetite for other male companions, then I am very happy," replied Ivan acerbically.

"That's exactly what it means, baby. I now have all I want right here," assured Svetlana.

Ivan was very happy in this moment, but by no means did he totally believe Svetlana. She had strayed too many times for him to believe she could quit cold turkey. He was also not sure that he could keep his promise to raise Anastasia on this enchanted island. The invasion of a country neighboring Russia, to satisfy Putin's thirst for the blood and destruction, had begun over a month ago. Each new day, the war brought more death and atrocities. The world was beginning to react against Russia's aggression in various ways. One such way was to impact the privileged lives of Russia's elite. By seizing the money and property of the Russian oligarchs, the world hoped that this elite group would turn against Putin. The secret body that ruled Russia behind the scenes was furious with Putin, and was currently creating their plan to deal with the situation. The urgency of the situation had caused the group to cease their operations in America, and to recall all Russian operatives. Ivan had received information from his superiors within this enigmatic group that he was on the list of Russian oligarchs who would be attacked financially. The Vladmelovs had assets all around the world, and Ivan needed to find out exactly which assets they were trying to seize. If the extensive private complex on Sardinia were targeted, he and his family would have to leave immediately and return to the safety of Russia. Ivan did not see the need to share this information with Svetlana until he was able to obtain more definitive details. For now they would ignore the information and bask in the love of their new child, Anastasia.

    Their jet landed in Olbia and the pilots taxied the plane to the luxurious terminal decorated especially for Sardinia's distinguished, affluent visitors. Outside were three black SUVs with Ivan's drivers and security team. The Vladmelovs exited the jet while their team filled the SUVs with their belongings that they had brought from America. The ride to Portisco was breathtaking, making it a very pleasant twenty-minute journey. Their enormous complex was just outside the town, and overlooked the Mediterranean Sea. Before heading to their home, Svetlana wanted to drive by the famous marina to give Anastasia a glimpse of their yacht, which was one of her favorite luxuries. Ivan had surprised her with this floating mansion a few years back on their anniversary.

"There she is, the 'Lady S'," Svetlana whispered to Anastasia as she pointed towards the yacht docked within its slip in the famous Marina.

Sailing enthusiasts from around the world loved to sail into and around Portisco, the gem of the Emerald Coast. Svetlana felt so alive when she was on this island. As she looked out over the marina, something caught her wandering eye. Their yacht was occupied by its all male crew, and they were currently cleaning the yacht. The crew was dressed in only their Canadian sausage holders, as she so aptly called them. She simply could not take her eyes off the Captain as he bent over to wipe down the yacht. Svetlana had never taken notice of this man before, but today her curiosity piqued. When they finally left the marina area, Svetlana snapped back to reality. Ivan had no clue what she was looking at because her lustful eyes were covered by a pair of extravagantly expensive sun glasses.

While they were en route to Sardinia, Ivan had made sure his staff had converted one of their rooms into a nursery for Anastasia. He hired an interior decorator on the island and told her to spare no expense when outfitting his child's new room. Ivan could not wait for Svetlana to see the surprise he had created for her and Anastasia. The caravan of SUVs entered the well-guarded complex, parking in front of the grand entrance to the main house. The flowers, in the floral garden overlooking the Mediterranean Sea, were swaying in the cool, soft sea breeze. Ivan led his family directly to their child's new room. When they entered, the first thing they saw was a beautiful crib. There was a soft canopy that draped from the ceiling, and appeared to float around the top of the crib. Ivan was pleased with the designer's finished product.

"Oh Ivan, this is absolutely beautiful. Anastasia, look at the surprise Daddy gave us," Svetlana said, then gave her husband a long, passionate kiss.

This was the life Ivan had longed for, but he was still saddened by his thoughts. He remained riddled with doubt over the sincerity of his wife's commitment to their marriage. He had no doubt of her steadfast commitment to their new daughter, Anastasia, but he was very skeptical of her loyalty to him. Only time would tell. He had to put these thoughts out of his mind and get down to the task of securing the grounds. The security team must be put on heightened alert, and Ivan needed an update on the world's progress concerning him and other Russian tycoons.

CHAPTER 39

Red called a buddy who he had served with in Afghanistan and who now worked in the United States Justice Department. Red explained his daughter's kidnapping, and asked if an APB alert could be activated up and down the East coast for the black SUV. He also explained the focus should be on air travel, because the crooks were headed to Sardinia.

Lily had the foresight to memorize the license plate when she had first arrived at the cabin. Red provided his friend the plate number, and a description of all the people in the vehicle. His friend assured Red that the Justice Department would do everything in its power to locate the vehicle, and his baby daughter.

Lily, and the organization she worked for, had arranged for a military chopper to pick them up at a small, local airstrip. From there they would be transported to Loring Air Force Base. Loring had been long since decommissioned, but its airstrips could still used when sensitive situations arose. There would be a private jet awaiting their arrival at Loring. This jet would fly them and all their gear to Sardinia. The flight would take eight to nine hours, which would give Lily time to brief the team with mission details. The team would consist of Lily, Red, Zach and Jack, if they all agreed to be part of this rescue. Without any hesitation, the entire team was onboard and would do whatever was necessary to get Elmear home safely.

Lily told Red there was just enough time for him to go into town and explain the situation to his wife, Alannah. Naturally, Zach wanted to explain the mission to Layla as well, and Jack needed to do the same for his loved ones. All three men headed to town in the battered truck that had just transported them through the woods. Lily went back inside the cabin and made sure the guard was still properly secured until officials could arrive and place him under arrest. She left the cabin and headed to the airstrip to meet the chopper, and wait for the other three to say their goodbyes.

Jack dropped Red and Zach off at the hospital where Alannah was recuperating and Layla was standing guard. Jack made his way through town to the Sheriff's station. He wanted to make phone calls to his loved ones, try to connect with Asadi to give him further information, and locate a car that they could take to the airstrip.

Red's stomach sank when he entered Alannah's hospital room. He had to tell her that Elmear was still a captive, and was headed to another country. Alannah looked up at Red and her eyes welled up with tears when she noticed he did not have Elmear.

"Please tell me she's still alive. Please God, let my baby be alive," Alannah begged out loud.

Zach motioned to Layla to come out into the hallway with him.

"Let's go to the empty waiting room down the hall so we can talk," Zach said to Layla.

"She is alive my love," Red whispered into Alannah's ear as the two hugged and wept.

"Ivan Vladmelov is more than just a rich man investing in businesses around the world. Also, his wife Svetlana not only worked for our government, but she also works for a secret Russian group. Ivan works for the same group and they were sent to America as part of a planned mission to bring chaos and turmoil to America. They took our child as a bargaining chip. Lily Crenna works for a similar American secret group of people. I don't know much about these two groups, but Calian Nakai is involved and informed Lily to trust us. If Calian trusts her, then I trust her as well. Lily had information that the Vladmelovs have taken our daughter to their home in Sardinia. Lily and her superiors have devised a plan to get us to Sardinia and get our daughter back. Zach, Jack and I have to leave immediately and meet her at the small airstrip just outside of town," explained Red.

"We need Elmear back, but please understand I need you back as well. I have so many more questions, but I trust you and Calian. Please go and make sure you and our daughter come home safely to me," Alannah replied to Red still, sobbing.

Zach described the situation to Layla who was both scared and supportive at the same time. "Watch your back and make sure Red has his head on straight before you hit the battle zone. He is full of emotion and needs you to ground him. You keep these people safe and get your ugly ass home to me. Once this is over, you my love are taking me back to Sardinia to vacation on that beautiful island," Layla said.

"Deal! I love you," Zach replied as they left the room to get Red and head out.

Red was headed out into the hallway. Layla stopped him, gave him a hug and whispered, "I will keep Alannah safe no matter what. You fight your angry emotions, and work with everyone as a team to bring your daughter and this team back safely!"

Red winked, caught up with Zach and the two left the hospital. Jack had briefed Asadi, who wanted to come, but knew he could be more helpful securing the town for Red. Asadi found Jack a vehicle to use, and he was outside the hospital waiting for Red and Zach when they came outside. The three men left town and headed to the airstrip, which was about a fifteen-minute drive. The car ride was very quiet as each man thought about what might happen in Sardinia.

The large chopper was already in place when they arrived. Its powerful blades were running, and ready to take off at a moment's notice. Jack, Red and Zach exited the car and headed towards the chopper, being sure they ducked low as they ran under the massive, spinning rotors. When they reached the side door, it slid open and to their surprise, Calian Nakai extended his hand to help each of them jump into the chopper.

"It's good to see you my friends! Let's go get your daughter back," Calian said as the chopper left the ground.

CHAPTER 40

The cyberattack that had created turmoil all over America had finally been stopped. The NSA team had been making progress in shutting the hack down, and Randy's destruction of the hardware had put the finishing touches on the destruction of the genius security breach. The intended outcome of the attack had been altered when the Russians had gotten involved. Luckily, the premature end to the computer ambush had thwarted the Russians' plan to put America into turmoil so that normalcy would never return. The intended outcome from the unknown society controlling America had been achieved.

There had been chaos; there had been mayhem. Americans felt despair; Americans had blamed their government. Americans were ready for change, and they were ready to put the government officials on notice. Money would begin to flow again, the power grids would return to full power, and food processing plants would be rebuilt. The government would not return to normal. "Power to the people" would become the norm as opposed to a slogan to promote change. This would not occur overnight, but the winds of change were blowing, and America would return better than ever.

Asadi and Logan saw that anger was subsiding from observing the people around town. They had started to help each other, and work together. Asadi was still outside the computer repair shop, and had been discussing what should be done next with Logan. Out of the corner of his eye, he suddenly noticed that Lily Crenna was walking toward the crime scene. From what little Jack had told him about Lily, Asadi was very surprised to see her in town. He thought she was on her way to Sardinia with Red and the other members of the team.

"Lily, what are you doing here?" Asadi asked.

"When he spoke to you, Red was not yet aware that I would not be on the flight to help save his child. I would have been a liability to the team, and that is not something I, or my superiors, were willing to accept. I was raised to serve America in ways you could never imagine. I bore my children in the name of my country. Randy and Abigail are my children and a mother cannot quell the natural instincts, and feelings, motherhood brings. I would not be able to concentrate on such an important mission knowing my own children are in such dire trouble. In essence, I betrayed Randy and Abigail as a mother to make sure my mission to correct America's path was successful. This is not a good feeling, and one I will carry with me until I die. I also feel a sense of responsibility to this town and its people. These people were good to me, were good to my family, and I will not just abandon them. Calian understood this, and allowed me to exit this mission, set some things straight in town and wait for my next assignment," Lily explained.

"I cannot imagine what you are going through. I am here if I can help you in any way. I'm going to start by being brutally honest with you about your children. Abigail has passed away. In a fit of rage she drove her car through the front of the computer repair shop, and fatally shot Boris multiple times. Randy confessed to his role in the conspiracy, and was cooperating with authorities. Since his crimes were against the United States government, he was taken by the FBI, who is now in charge of this investigation," Asadi replied in a somber manner.

"Good! The FBI will be instructed to release him to our people," Lily thought to herself. She knew that she would never see him again, that he would live out his life in anonymity and seclusion, but he would remain alive, which she took comfort in knowing.

"I need to make my way to the logging company's executive offices. Without Paul and Randy, I am the only one left to be sure this company stays alive. I must find a way to bring it back to its glory days, and find a successor who will take over running the business. I don't want to sell to a stranger or conglomerate. Paul has a brother who might be willing to take it over, which would keep it in the Crenna family. Its success and future are important to me, because I want this town to continue to thrive. It's probably the last good thing I will be able to do to honor my daughter, and son's lives," Lily said tearfully.

CHAPTER 41

Red, Zach and Jack were all happy to see Calian, and Calian was just as glad to see the three of them. The four men had gone through some very stressful times together in the past few years. Calian slid the chopper door shut, and gave the pilot the signal to take off. Zach had an uneasy feeling about this man whom they had fought side by side with in the China-American war. Calian did not seem as sincere and warm as Zach remembered him being.

"It's so good to see you again. By now I'm sure you have noticed the absence of Lily Crenna. I did not feel that Lily would be a good fit for this assignment. I have brought Mikhail to help us retrieve Red's daughter, Elmear. Mikhail is very qualified in the art of war, and has worked in a cohesive operative unit to achieve a specific goal," explained Calian in a cold calculated manner.

Zach's senses had become heightened when he saw Mikhail on the plane. When Zach heard that the stranger would be part of the rescue team, he became resolute to watch Mikhail's every move.

"We are minutes from Loring Air Force base where we will disembark and immediately board our private jet. The jet is outfitted with technology that will allow us to go over the plan using video of the actual sight in Portisco, Sardinia," Calian outlined to the group.

The chopper landed, and everyone boarded the luxurious private jet waiting on the runway. Zach was the last one to board, following Mikhail onto the plane. The co-pilot closed the doors, took her position in the cockpit, and the plane started cruising down the runway, eventually floating off the ground. Now that they were in flight, Calian started the mission prep. An overhead screen lowered from the plane ceiling, and Calian flipped on the projection system. The image of a beautiful complex, nestled amongst the cliffs, and overlooking the Mediterranean Sea, appeared on the screen. Calian began briefing the group.

"This is the Vladmelov complex located in Portisco, Sardinia. At first glance, it is a massive complex, but our focus is only on the section we are showing on the screen. We have confirmation that

Ivan, and his wife have arrived. The arrival was sudden, so only one section of the complex was readied for their stay. Through satellite surveillance, we have seen no more than eight guards in the area. This fact could change at any moment because Ivan will add security as he learns of the world's effort to seize Russian magnates' assets."

Before Calian could explain, Red spoke up, "What the hell does this have to do with getting my daughter?"

"Calm down Red! This mission has two goals: the retrieval of Elmear, and setting the stage for Sardinian officials to seize everything Ivan owns on the island. I had to combine these missions as it was not possible to organize such an effort to retrieve one hostage," replied Calian Nakai.

Red and Zach looked at each other with both disgust and fear. They wondered who this man was, and how such a serene, caring man could morph into a cold-hearted human. Zach's fears were now a reality; Calian Nakai was not the man they had known before. They had no choice but to settle in and listen to the master plan.

"The Sardinian authorities, with the Italian government's blessing, have given us a twenty-four hour window to extract Elmear and leave the country without interference from local law enforcement. They basically are allowing us to plow the field for them to come in and tell the world they have seized Vladmelov's assets. By seizing this oligarch's large cache of valuables, the world will know Sardinia stood against the Russian atrocities currently underway as they continue their attack on a neighboring country."

"You are the four operatives who will be in the field; I will stay in the command center coordinating the activity. Red and Jack will enter through the rear of the building by making their way through the rough mountainous terrain behind the complex. Zach and Mikhail will enter through the front gate, which will require killing any guards at that site. All weapons will include silencing mechanisms, and Jack will have a sniper rifle. Once inside the main house, Jack will make his way to the roof to handle anything that happens in the area that might be out of the view of Zach and Mikhail," Calian droned on in a militaristic manner.

The projector images had changed from the property overview, to the rear terrain, to the interior of the home, to the rooftop arrangement, and finally the front of the main home. The front of the home had about twenty feet of clear space that ended at a four to five-foot wall of stone. This stone had been sculpted into the shape of a long trough that contained rich soil and beautiful flowers. Just behind the flowers was a high ledge leading straight down to the Mediterranean Sea.

Zach wanted to talk to Red and Jack in private, which would not be possible inside this luxury tube flying through the air. There was nowhere to go to talk secretly, except the lavatory. Surely the two could not go to the lavatory together without raising eyebrows. The three had to memorize the terrain and the plan details, then trust their instincts that had carried them through Afghanistan.

Zach decided to speak directly with Calian to try and get to the bottom of his altered persona. Zach was not one to beat around the bush, so he went over to Calian and hit the issue head on.

"Calian, what happened to the man we knew from the war? You were the man to lead America out of the war with your passionate patriotism. You always spoke with passion and respect for the people you wanted to serve. Now, you sound like a governmental robot. What happened?" Zach asked.

"I became disenchanted with the swamp-infested government, and the progressive groups all over the country wreaking havoc and destruction on our society. They are the minority, but due to their solidarity, they are leading the country down a dangerous path. I was asked to join this elite group to run the country behind the scenes, behind the view of the idiots elected to run our country. This has made me less compassionate, I know, but it does not change my resolve to bring America back to a peaceful, caring society. Actually I would like you and your team to come work for us. You are exactly the type of patriots and soldiers we need to move our agenda forward. Before you say no, because you think I have changed for the worse, give it some thought and talk with Red and Jack," replied Calian in a sincere moment.

    The men were quiet, each studying in their own way, except for Mikhail. He appeared disinterested in the entire mission. His mannerisms were very aloof as he ignored the group and was more interested in sleeping than in preparing. Zach's gut was raging with instinct … instinct telling him Mikhail was not on their side, and Calian's devotion to Elmear's return was in question. He had to remain alert; they had to succeed with this critical, personal mission!

CHAPTER 42

Svetlana had slept in late because Anastasia had had a fitful night in her new surroundings. Svetlana held her, fed her and soothed her without feeling frustrated or angered about her lack of sleep. She loved her daughter, and felt sad that Anastasia might be scared and stressed over her unfamiliar home. She finally settled and was still sleeping, so Svetlana mirrored her schedule.

Ivan had been up for hours working on multiple important tasks, from business dealings, to security concerns, to trying to determine if the world would be coming after his assets. One of his biggest security concerns for the day was the protection of Anastasia and Svetlana on their shopping trip to town later. If the Vladmelov's assets had become a target to the world, so would his family.

"Bring in two more armed guards to accompany us to town later today. I don't want to use any people who are providing protection around the property," Ivan ordered his chief of security.

Ivan had walked back into the main house to the sounds of Anastasia crying. Hearing her in distress, Ivan then headed to the nursery, so he could tend to Anastasia. He had hoped this would allow Svetlana more time to sleep, while giving him some alone time with his child. When Ivan arrived at the nursery door, Anastasia was already cradled in Svetlana's arms. Her crying had stopped, which indicated to Ivan that hopefully the baby was bonding with her new mother.

"Good morning love. Will you help me get our little bundle of joy ready for today's adventures? We have to get her some new clothes and diapers first. We only have this one outfit for her to wear. Will you change her diaper while I gather her clothes?" Svetlana asked her husband.

Ivan's eyes got wide with fear. This was a man who had killed or maimed others throughout this life. He now stood petrified over this helpless little girl. His knees were knocking and his hands were trembling as they moved downward to begin removing the diaper. Svetlana stood in the background watching this comical, but touching moment in their new family's life.

"Watch while I change her diaper Ivan. There's no need to be afraid. Just be gentle, and softly talk to her while you are changing the dirty diaper," explained Svetlana.

Svetlana finished dressing Anastasia, then handed her to Ivan. He held his daughter with pride. Ivan walked her around the house and introduced Anastasia to each and every room. Suddenly Ivan's phone rang, which caused him to relinquish his baby time back to his wife.

"Ivan, we are a family now. You need to work less, so you can spend most of your time with us. Please, I want us to raise our child together," Svetlana pleaded.

"Right now I have some pressing issues that I did not want you to know about. Putin's misstep into war has created hatred for Russians all over the world. The assets of most Russian elite are at risk of being seized by various countries in an attempt to cripple the Russian economy. If they come for our wealth, we may also be in danger, so I am preparing for this possibility. Be patient, and when this passes I will spend all my time with you, and Anastasia," Ivan replied lovingly.

The phone call was from Ivan's security chief who had called to inform him that the two additional guards were on the way, and would be there soon. Ivan had taken Anastasia from Svetlana once again so that she could shower and dress for their trip to town. Ivan intended to go with them, as long as everything remained calm.

CHAPTER 43

The captain announced that the private jet had just started its final descent into Olbia. The men onboard had started their final prep for the mission. They had packed their gear into touristy-looking backpacks, and their loaded pistols were hidden underneath their clothing. Red and Jack would be seen by the public more than the others, so they upped their touristy look by hanging a camera around their neck.

"Outside the airport, there will be a limo driver waiting for us to arrive. He will be holding a sign with my last name on it. He will be driving us to our destination in a white limo bus, which will also double as our command center. In addition, the driver is one of our operatives, and he and I will operate the command center. Put your comm pieces into your ear and let's make sure we can hear each other. These are designed to assist us in communicating with each other," explained Calian.

The captain instructed everyone to sit down because the jet was about to land. During the very smooth landing, Zach noticed that a fidgety Mikhail had been approached by Calian. The two conversed quietly, and quickly, obviously trying not to draw attention to their discussion. The plane taxied to the terminal where everyone disembarked. Just as Calian had described, the driver was holding a "Nakai" sign, making it easy to locate him. They all followed the driver to the small bus and began their journey to the Vladmelov complex. During the ride, quiet came over the inside of the bus. The reality of what was about to happen had taken over their thoughts. The beauty of the island was overshadowed by the coming battle. Red continued to push his emotions to the background, to be sure he was focused on only the return of Elmear.

"Red and Jack, your drop point is coming up soon. Remember, once we drop you off, you will have about ten minutes to get into position. Once you are in position, signal us via the comm system. Keep your heads in the game and watch your back!" Calian announced.

Soon after Calian's pep talk, the limo driver pulled over to drop off the two men. Red and Jack gave the thumbs up signal as they exited the vehicle to begin their hike. This was a popular tourist spot, with hiking paths going through the mountainous region of the island. Jack and Red gave the appearance of avid tourists. The hiking path came to a junction, with the crowds of tourists using the right hand path leading from the area. Red and Jack casually took the path leading to the left. Once they were out of the sight of others, the two began to sprint up the hill. They slowed when they caught sight of the Vladmelov property. There were two guards overlooking the hills and valleys behind the many buildings that made up Ivan's complex. Before they could move up the hill into position, these two guards had to be eliminated. Jack unpacked and then assembled the sniper rifle that was inside his backpack. While Jack was preparing the rifle, Red scoured the area for the best vantage point for the sniper.

    Jack settled into the small secluded nook that Red had located. It provided him a place to rest the rifle to assure it remained steady while he prepared to shoot. This would not be a simple shot, so he took a moment to study the guards' movements. There was one point where the guards walked towards each other and stood next to each other. This would be the point Jack would eliminate one, turn ever so slightly and take out the other guard before he had time to alert others of the attack. The time had come; Jack squeezed the trigger; the rifle moved slightly to the left and Jack squeezed the trigger for the second time. As both guards fell to the ground, Jack rose, grabbed his backpack, and carried the rifle as the two ascended the hill to their final destination. Within moments, Red and Jack had arrived at the rear entrance of the main home.

"In position," Red alerted the others over the comm system.

From the front, the Vladmelov estate was somewhat secluded from others, but still had walkways and roads that allowed people to witness the beauty and grandeur of the island and the vast complex. Naturally, there was a gate with one guard at the entrance. Just past the entrance was a scenic stop that allowed vehicles and pedestrians a view of the Mediterranean Sea. Calian's people had located a chink in the complex's armor, and this is how Zach and Mikhail would enter the grounds from the front. The driver pulled into the scenic overlook where Zach and Mikhail exited the bus, and immediately began snapping pictures of the wondrous surroundings. They waited a few moments until the crowd thinned a little. The two moved to the right of the stone wall that prevented people from falling into the sea. They moved into a basin protected by a small clump of trees. The trees followed the hill that the two would travel out of the basin, and would help keep them hidden. They crouched low to the ground when they reached the top of the hill. In addition to the guard at the front gate, there were two others who made up the security team out front.

"In position out front," Zach relayed through the comm.

"Roger that. Mission is now a go!" relayed Calian from the command center.

CHAPTER 44

Svetlana was dressed and had taken Anastasia from Ivan so he could attend to a few business items before they left for the day's shopping adventure. Ivan headed to his office that was located in the rear portion of the main house, while Svetlana finished getting Anastasia's diaper bag ready.

Having eliminated the two rear guards, Red and Jack were able to enter the home without being noticed. Once inside the house, the two men moved with precision and caution. Knowing there were three guards inside, or on the roof of the home, Jack and Red's gun-wielding hands were outstretched, and their bodies swayed back and forth scanning for the guards. Like clockwork, they moved deeper into the home. Suddenly Jack turned left down a hallway and headed toward the roof entrance. He reached the roof entrance, crouched down and slowly opened the door, peaking every so carefully before going outside. The guard saw Jack first, but Jack was able to shoot first. The shot was silent, but accurate as the body fell lifeless to the ground. Jack continued outside, carefully checking the rest of the roof and staying low to avoid being seen by anyone on the ground. He worked his way toward the front of the house, and found a position to rest his sniper rifle and secure the area below.

"Roof is secure, and one more guard is down," Jack informed the others.

Each man took note of the body count. Three guards down, two remained inside the house, two remained in the front being watched by Zach and Mikhail, and the last guard was manning the gate at the driveway entrance.

Red continued further into the interior of the main house. All of a sudden he could hear footsteps that seemed to be coming from the hallway. Red turned and walked back to where Jack had gone down the hallway to enter the roof access. He stood quietly and listened as the footsteps got closer and closer. Half of the guard's body had become visible to Red. Red wrapped his arms around the guard's neck and put one hand over his mouth. He enlisted the use of a military choke hold that would render someone unconscious before killing them. He moved the guard's body into a nearby empty room, had put a gag in his mouth and then wire-tied his hands behind him. To keep the man immobile, Red threw him on the bed, sat the man upright with his arms behind him, and zip tied his arms to the headboard.

"One guard inside immobilized, but alive," Red informed the rest of the team.

As Red re-entered the hallway, he heard another visitor coming his way. He closed the door and had left enough of a gap for him to see who was headed in his direction. Red watched a man enter the room on the other side of the hall slightly offset from where he was located. Once the stranger closed the door, Red slowly made his way to the other room. Rather than barge in guns blazing, Red carefully opened the door hoping to catch the occupant off guard. He came face to face with Ivan Vladmelov, who remained quite calm even though a gun was pointed towards his head. Red closed the door and moved closer to Ivan.

"I should just kill you where you stand, you son of a bitch. I have dreamed of this moment where you beg for your life. Where is my daughter and be very careful how you answer," Red said as he shook with anger.

"She is safe with her new mother, my wife Svetlana. Killing me will not save your daughter, but you do as you wish," Ivan boldly answered.

"In these few seconds, I've realized that death would be too good for you. You will be secured and the Sardinian authorities will take everything you own and you will rot in prison knowing you have nothing left in this world. But, I will tell you I will have no trouble killing your wife to get my daughter back. So as you sit here bound and gagged, you give that some thought, little man," Red said in anger.

"SVETLANA …," Ivan yelled, which then was followed by, *"Crack, crack,"* when Red fired two shots, hitting Ivan in each leg. He fell to the floor and yelled in agony before Red could jump on top of him and render him unconscious with the butt of his gun.

"Ivan subdued, but yelled to alert people of danger. Watch your backs. Svetlana may be on the run any moment," Red said into the comm system as he finished making sure Ivan would not be able to escape. A noise behind him caused Red to spin around. As he turned, a guard began to raise her gun to fire at Red. Red dove to the floor, aimed his weapon and shot three times in her direction before hitting the carpet. The guard fell backwards into the hallway, landing upright against the wall, then her body slid to the floor lifeless.

"Second guard inside is dead," Red told the team.

Svetlana headed to the front door with Elmear in her arms, and all hell broke loose in the front of the house. Zach and Mikhail split up, with Zach remaining near the front gate to take care of the guard. The two other security people out front converged to help Svetlana. Jack took them both out shooting from his perch on the rooftop. That meant seven of the eight security people were out of the fight. Zach was making his way to the front gate when he noticed a car coming into the complex.

"Vehicle just entered the front gate with two people inside," Zach indicated through the comm.

Zach made sure the guard would never let anyone through the gate again, and then began heading up the driveway following the vehicle. When they saw the dead bodies near the front of the home, the car stopped short of the house, and the two occupants got out with their guns drawn. Jack took aim and eliminated them both very quickly. All of a sudden Mikhail screamed in horror, "That was my wife you just killed getting out of the car." Mikhail started shooting rapid fire in Jack's direction. When the clip was emptied, he reloaded and continued to fire. As the last shot left his pistol, Mikhail's body jerked forward, and he fell from the rock ledge he was standing on. As he fell, Calian appeared from a position behind Mikhail, and was lowering his pistol.

Just as Mikhail fell, Svetlana ran out the door with the baby in her arms. Red was next to come out the front door. Svetlana continued to run towards the ledge looking over the Mediterranean Sea. She stopped short of the ledge and started yelling.

"You have two choices and only two choices. You let the two of us drive off into the sunset to live another day, or I jump taking both of us to our death."

Zach froze in a position just to Svetlana's left, and she was precariously holding Anastasia on her left side. Red stood facing Svetlana with his gun pointing in her direction, but he knew he could not fire.

Jack knew what to do, and spoke carefully into the comm, "Red, trust me. Lower your gun to show her good faith. When I shoot, her body will shudder forward before arching backwards off the cliff. In that forward movement Zach will have enough time to sprint in, and grab Elmear. I will shoot on three and you should begin moving on one, Zach."

Red trusted his brothers with his life, but hesitated because this was his daughter's life. There really was no choice, so he lowered his weapon.

"One," Jack uttered and Zach sprung into action.

"Two, three," was followed by *"Pop, Pop!"* Svetlana arched forward and Zach dove through the air and grabbed Elmear just before Svetlana fell backwards into the sea.

Mikhail was not dead, and during the commotion had risen up enough to fire three shots before he collapsed in death. All three bullets hit Zach just before he grabbed Elmear.

It took only seconds for these soldiers to realize Elmear was safe, but Zach was dead.

CHAPTER 45

Their speedy exit from Sardinia was necessary because they had left death and destruction all over Ivan's complex. The authorities gave them the time they had agreed upon, but they never expected this much carnage.

The private jet was loaded and immediately took off for Loring Air Force Base in America. Red sat holding Elmear, and cried as he stared at the body bag lying on the floor across from him. His best friend, his comrade in arms, had given up his life to save Elmear. Jack felt he was responsible for Zach's death, because it was he who initiated the plan. Each man suffered in silence over the death of their brave friend. Suddenly Red stood and handed Elmear to Jack. He drew his gun and aimed it at Calian's head.

"You have become the coldest son of a bitch I have ever met. You killed Zach. You brought Mikhail into this mission and Zach knew something was not right with that decision. You had ulterior motives and now our friend is dead because of you!"

"I had to know if Mikhail was one of us or not. The only way to tell was to put him into this sensitive position. You have no idea what important work we do and my decision was necessary," Nakai replied.

"You have changed, and the friend I knew has turned into a monster. A monster that I should kill here and now," Red was interrupted when Jack said, "Red, not here and not now. You don't want your daughter to witness any more tragedy. Come here my friend. Take your daughter and let's go home. Let's take our friend home in honor."

The silent flight landed at Loring, and Jack arranged for their transportation back to Crenna. They wanted nothing to do with Nakai and sent him on his way. When they reached Crenna, Layla began sobbing watching from the hospital room window, as Red, Jack, and Elmear exited the car followed by a body bag. She knew Zach was gone and her knees wilted from under her. The three made their way to Alannah's room where Red handed Elmear to Alannah. Red grabbed Layla and hugged her, whispering into her ear, "I am so sorry Layla. He died saving Elmear, and I will never be able to thank him for this."

The next few weeks were filled with heavy sadness and happiness. Alannah was overjoyed to have Elmear in her arms, but the sadness she felt for Layla was immense. Layla felt numb and lost without the light of her life. She placed no blame. Zach was a man of honor and would have done anything for his family and friends. He lived with this mantra and died with this conviction. Zach would have been honored that he had helped to save Elmear.

Red and Alannah decided to remain in Crenna, and tried to convince Layla to move there as well. It was too soon for that, but she assured them she would give it some thought. The twins were born and the Kelly family grew to five overnight. Naming these twin boys was easy and was completely Alannah's decision. The first boy that arrived would be the oldest Kelly child, and was named Liam Junior.

The second twin boy was named Zach and would be raised to be an honorable, brave man just like his namesake.

THE END!

FINAL THOUGHT

I wanted to once again thank my wife Sheri for her undying support throughout this process. Sheri has devoted quite a bit of time to helping me through this writing process. She is also an aspiring artist and drew the picture on the following page to capture the Crenna cabin where Elmear's life changed dramatically.

I would also like to thank my entire orbit of family, friends and everyone else who have read the Morrelli series, for their support and help in my writing endeavor. With the death of Zach, I feel it is time to end the series, which does not necessarily mean the end of my writing. I don't know what might be next, but I look forward to the adventure.

Thank you again for your support and guidance.

RC Merrell

Made in the USA
Middletown, DE
25 July 2022